PRAISE FOR

THE
GUARDIAN
~HERD~
STARFIRE

"Chock-full of adventure and twists, making it difficult to put down. Readers will be clamoring for the next book."   —*SLJ*

"Alvarez's world is lush with description and atmosphere, and her premise has much to offer. . . . Fans of animal fantasies should find it enjoyable."   —*Publishers Weekly*

"Will prove popular with both animal-lovers and fantasy fans. A good choice for reluctant readers. The clever resolution will get kids psyched for more tales from the Guardian Herd."
                                        —ALA *Booklist*

"From page one, Jennifer Lynn Alvarez weaves an epic tale of a doomed black Pegasus foal named Star, whose race against time will lift the reader on the wings of danger and destiny, magic and hope. It's a world I did not want to leave, and neither will you."
                    —Peter Lerangis, *New York Times* bestselling
                                author of the Seven Wonders series

Also by Jennifer Lynn Alvarez
The Guardian Herd: Stormbound

THE
GUARDIAN
HERD

STARFIRE

BY
JENNIFER LYNN ALVAREZ

HARPER
An Imprint of HarperCollinsPublishers

Library of Congress Cataloging-in-Publication Data
Alvarez, Jennifer Lynn.
    Starfire / by Jennifer Lynn Alvarez. — First edition.
        pages cm. — (Guardian Herd)
    Summary: "Star is prophesized to become the most powerful winged horse in Anok on his first birthday, but he must first overcome his malformed wings that make him unable to fly and threats from the leaders of the five herds"— Provided by publisher.
    ISBN 978-0-06-228607-9 (pbk.)
    [1. Fantasy. 2. Adventure and adventurers—Fiction. 3. Animals, Mythical—Fiction. 4. Animals—Abnormalities—Fiction.] I. Title.
PZ7.A4797St 2014   2014001890
[Fic]—dc23   CIP
                                                                             AC

15 16 17 18 19   CG/OPM   10 9 8 7 6 5 4 3 2 1
❖
First paperback edition, 2015

FOR MY FAMILY, TWO-LEGGED AND FOUR

TABLE OF CONTENTS

And sometimes, when you fall, you fly.

Neil Gaiman, *The Sandman, Vol. 6: Fables and Reflections*

SUN HERD

The Black Foal:

STAR—solid-black colt with black feathers, white star on
forehead

Over-stallion:

THUNDERWING—dark-bay stallion with vibrant crimson
feathers, black mane and tail, wide white blaze, two hind
white socks

Lead Mare:

SILVERCLOUD—light-gray mare with silver feathers, white
mane and tail, four white socks

Captains:

OAKFIRE—sable-gray stallion with copper feathers, black
mane and tail

JETFIRE—cream-colored stallion with turquoise feathers,
flaxen mane and tail, snip on nose

TWISTFIRE—red dun stallion with olive-green feathers,
dark-red mane and tail

ASHFIRE—gray dapple stallion with midnight-blue feathers,
dark-gray mane and tail, white blaze

Medicine Mare:

SWEETROOT—old chestnut pinto mare with dark-pink
feathers, chestnut mane and tail, white star

Leader of the Walkers:

GRASSWING—crippled palomino stallion with pale-green
feathers, flaxen mane and tail, blaze, one white front sock

Under-stallion:

HAZELWIND—buckskin stallion with jade feathers, black
mane and tail, big white blaze, two hind white socks

Mated Mares:

CRYSTALFEATHER—small chestnut mare with bright-blue
feathers, two front white socks, white strip on face

VIOLETSUN—gray pinto mare with violet feathers, dark-
gray mane and tail

ROWANWOOD—blue roan mare with dark yellow and blue
feathers, white mane and tail, two hind white socks

Single/Widowed Mares:

LIGHTFEATHER—small white mare with white feathers,
white ringlet tail, white mane. Star's dam. Born to Snow
Herd, adopted by Sun Herd. Deceased

DAWNFIR—bay Appaloosa mare with dark blue and white
feathers, black mane and tail

MAPLECLOUD—ambitious blond buckskin mare with dirt-colored feathers, black mane and tail

MOSSBERRY—elderly light-bay mare with dark-magenta feathers, black mane and tail, crescent moon on forehead and white snip on nose, two white hind anklets

Yearlings:

RIPPLEBREEZE—white yearling colt with dandelion-yellow feathers, white mane and tail

Foals:

MORNINGLEAF—elegant chestnut filly with bright-aqua feathers, flaxen mane and tail, four white socks, amber eyes, wide blaze

ECHOFROST—sleek silver filly with a mix of dark and light purple feathers, white mane and tail, one white sock

BUMBLEWIND—friendly bay pinto colt with gold feathers tipped in brown, black mane and tail, thin blaze on face

BRACKENTAIL—big brown colt with orange feathers, brown mane and tail, two hind white socks

STRIPESTORM—liver-chestnut colt with bright-yellow feathers, red mane and tail, thin white blaze

FLAMESKY—red roan filly with dark emerald and gold feathers

GRAYTHORN—palomino colt with violet-tipped gray feathers, thin white blaze, two white hind socks. Deceased colt of Grasswing, murdered by Rockwing

MOUNTAIN HERD

ROCKWING—over-stallion. Magnificent silver Appaloosa with dark blue and gray feathers, black mane and tail highlighted with white, one white front anklet

FROSTFIRE—captain. White with violet-tipped light-blue feathers, dark-gray mane and tail, and one blue eye. Born to Snow Herd, adopted by Mountain Herd

SNOW HERD

ICEWING—over-stallion. Older dark-silver stallion with powder-blue feathers, white mane, white ringlet tail, blue eyes, white star on forehead. Sire of Lightfeather

PETALCLOUD—lead mare. Power-seeking gray mare with violet feathers, silver mane and tail, one white sock, wide blaze on face

JUNGLE HERD

SNAKEWING—over-stallion. Bay with forest-green feathers, black mane and tail, one white sock

SMOKEWING—successor over-stallion. Bay Appaloosa with

brown-and-white-spotted feathers, black mane and tail, snip on nose

DESERT HERD

SANDWING—over-stallion. Proud palomino stallion with dark-yellow feathers, wide white blaze, one white sock

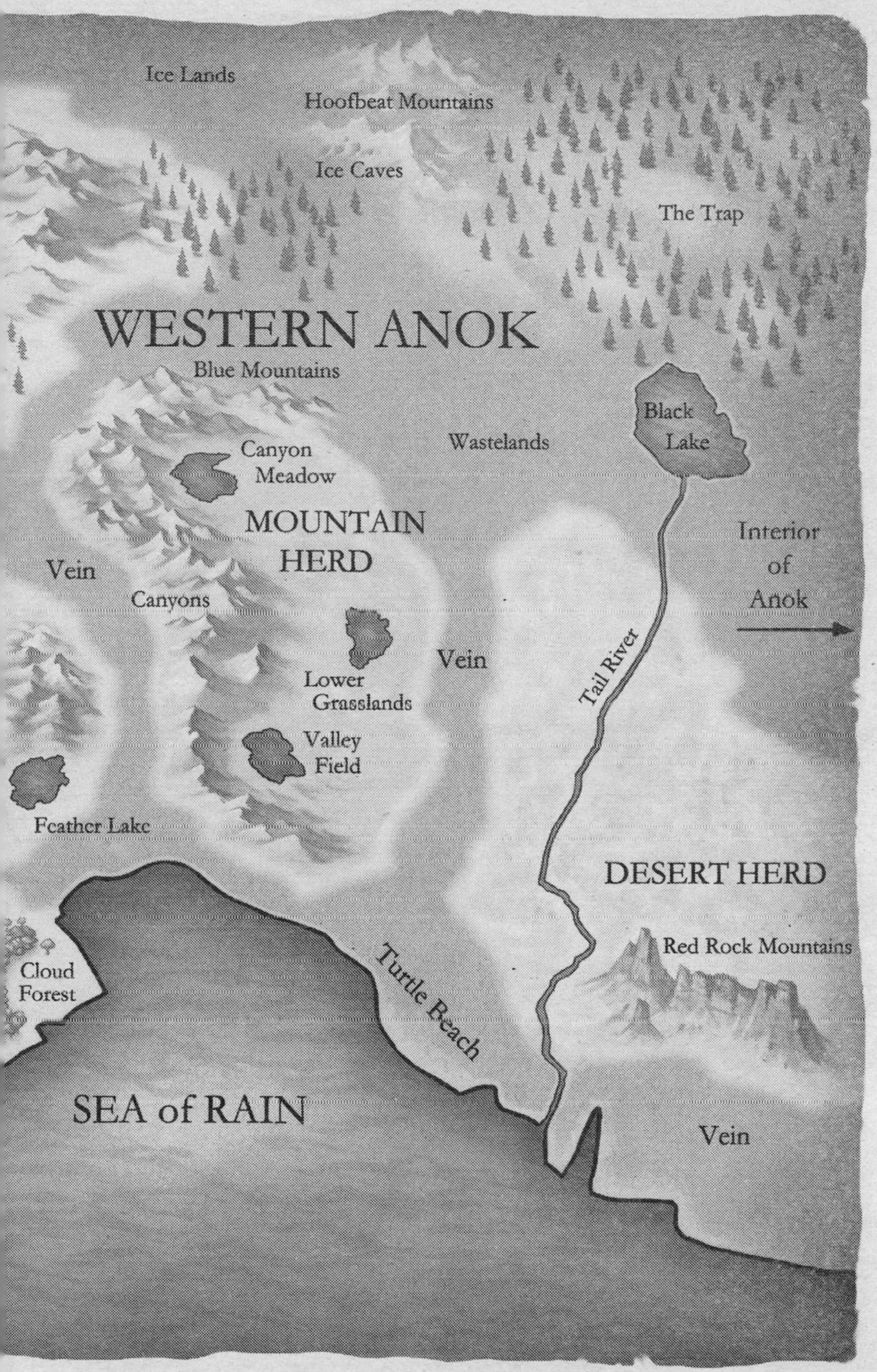

Ice Lands

Hoofbeat Mountains

Ice Caves

The Trap

WESTERN ANOK

Blue Mountains

Black Lake

Canyon
Meadow

Wastelands

MOUNTAIN
HERD

Vein

Canyons

Interior
of
Anok

Vein

Lower
Grasslands

Valley
Field

Tail River

Feather Lake

DESERT HERD

Red Rock Mountains

Cloud
Forest

Turtle Beach

SEA of RAIN

Vein

1

THE DEAL

STAR TROTTED THROUGH THE DENSE PINE FOREST, alone. He wanted to practice his flying where the herd couldn't see him. The sharp screech of a hawk drew his eyes skyward in time to see a band of pegasi pierce the drifting clouds. They swooped toward land impressively and then circled around, tapping wings as they passed one another in midair. They were Sun Herd yearlings, out with their flight instructor. Star reared, stretching toward them, trying to fly, but his giant wings hung off him like dead tree branches—useless.

He sagged against a coarse fir tree, already sweating. It was getting hotter each day, and soon it would be time to migrate to the cooler grasslands in the north. He looked up again and watched the yearlings soar in easy loops. They'd been flying since the day they were born. But he—his wings never worked. If he could just tuck them onto his back, he wouldn't look so foolish walking amid the Sun Herd steeds in the grasslands.

Familiar voices pierced the silence, wafting on the breeze from Feather Lake. Star pricked his ears.

"Look at me; I'm a dud like Star."

Star crept to the edge of the trees and peeked through the pine needles. He saw two colts, Stripestorm and Brackentail, playing on the shore. Stripestorm dropped his wings and walked back and forth, imitating and exaggerating the swing-necked gait of a common horse.

Star huffed softly and hung his head. Their joking was why he'd wanted to be alone.

Brackentail snorted. "No, *this* is Star." He collapsed his wings and trotted in a circle, bleating, "Mama? Where's my mama?"

Stripestorm squealed so hard he fell over.

Star turned, galloping angrily out of the forest, ears pinned, and rammed Brackentail. "Don't talk about my mother!" he cried. They tumbled, head over wings.

Brackentail came up with a mouth full of sand. "Get him," he shouted to Stripestorm, choking.

Stripestorm charged, flapping his bright-yellow wings for speed, and Star met him, teeth bared. Stripestorm kicked, smashing Star in the chest and knocking the breath out of him. Brackentail rolled over and took flight, and Stripestorm joined him. They hovered over Star's head and pummeled him from the air.

Star reared, snapping his jaws. Stripestorm lunged, and Star sank his teeth into the smaller colt's leg, tossing him to the ground. Stripestorm tumbled. "Ooof!"

Brackentail flew in, clubbing Star's cheek with his hoof. Lights burst behind Star's eyes, shattering his vision. He shook his head to clear it, wincing at the sharp pain between his ears.

Stripestorm galloped into the sky, then swooped down, gliding toward Star with hooves coiled. Star ducked just in time. "Come and get us," taunted Brackentail as the two flew circles over his head.

Star glared at the colts, who flew just out of his reach. Brackentail harassed all the foals in Sun Herd, but Star was his favorite target—maybe because Star had no mother to protect him, or maybe because Star was a dud, a pegasus who couldn't fly.

Star dodged their hooves as they took turns kicking him. The sharp edge of Brackentail's hoof sliced Star's shoulder, causing bright-red blood to run down his front leg. "Back off," said Star.

"Back off," they repeated, adding a mocking whine to their tone. Stripestorm punctuated their taunting with a kick to Star's flank, causing Star's leg to buckle. Star staggered toward the lake, lost his balance, and fell in.

The two colts landed and hooked their wings around each other, nickering and watching Star struggle.

The shore on this end of the lake was steep, and Star sank when a cramp seized his oversize wings. Bubbles burst from his lips as the spasm rolled from his shoulders to his tail. He drifted helplessly to the bottom, his lungs burning, his black legs kicking.

He was destined to become the most powerful pegasus in Anok, and here he was, sinking to the bottom of Feather Lake. He landed upside down, his legs pointing upward and swaying like reeds. It was dark and cold, like the night. Star tried to flip over, to save himself, but he was running out of air.

Prisms of color exploded around him, and he was sure it meant the Ancestors were here and coming to take him to the golden meadow. As he was accepting this fate, suddenly there was thrashing in the water, and bright feathers surrounded him. They took hold of him and dragged him to the surface. His muscle spasm began to dissipate, and as he surfaced, Star spread his wings, floating and gulping huge mouthfuls of air.

"We've got him," said a male voice.

Star blinked the water out of his eyes, hopeful that he would see his friends, or maybe a regretful Brackentail. Instead he saw four strange stallions looming over him. His heart bucked. The bright feathers he thought were those of Morningleaf or Echofrost were actually of his enemies!

Star quickly twisted out of their grasp and bolted, galloping off an embankment and thundering toward the woods.

Amused nickering followed him. "So the rumors are true," said one of the stallions to another, "the black foal can't fly."

A white steed glided past Star and landed in front of him. He had one blue eye and one brown eye. Star skidded on his haunches and turned, almost crashing into the chests of the other three. He'd never seen these pegasi before. He looked around, but Brackentail and Stripestorm were nowhere.

"You can't escape us," said the white steed.

Star's feathers stood on end, and he was breathing

hard, prancing. "What do you want with me?"

Two stallions, a gray and a buckskin, clamped their jaws at the base of Star's wings. Another, a pinto, spoke, but not to Star. "We're ready, Frostfire," he said to the white stallion.

The stallion kicked off, angling his violet-tipped blue feathers, hovering over Star's head. "Let's go before those two colts we scared off tell Thunderwing we're here."

"No!" Star screamed. Searing pain ripped through his shoulders as the stallions lifted him by the roots of his wings and carried him into the sky. Below him the trees shrank, and Feather Lake contracted into a mere blue swirl. He dangled between the two sweating stallions, their heavily muscled wings pumping in synchronized rhythm as they headed east—toward Mountain Herd's territory. Star's scattered thoughts gathered into one heart-pounding realization. They were taking him to Rockwing!

Star had to get away before they reached the Vein, for if he crossed that into Rockwing's territory, it was doubtful he would make it out again alive. He thrashed and managed to yank one wing out of the gray's mouth. The sudden shift caused the buckskin still holding him to cartwheel into a nosedive. The two of them spiraled toward the dry foothills, Star's free wing whipping uselessly in the wind. The speed of the drop, the thrill of the heights, and the fear of the landing coursed through his veins like liquid lightning. Was this what it felt like to fly? Star wondered.

Star turned his head and saw the white stallion, Frostfire, follow them. The stallion curved his wings, banking sharply, and plunged toward the falling pair. He caught up to them and snatched Star's loose wing in his teeth, stopping his fall. Frostfire and the gray stallion worked together to stabilize their captive and resume their flying altitude.

"What's wrong with you?" Frostfire shouted over the whistle of the wind.

Star pinned his ears and glanced back toward Sun Herd's territory, shrinking in the distance. The sky behind him was empty. Where was Thunderwing? Brackentail and Stripestorm should have arrived in Dawn Meadow by now and sounded the alarm. Star knew that as overstallion, Thunderwing could assemble his flying army in minutes.

The stallions held him so tight he could feel each of their individual teeth. The foothills were behind him now, and ahead was the Vein, the neutral seam that ran between each territory of the five herds. Star had never traveled outside his own Sun Herd's territory.

He struggled, more afraid of Rockwing than of falling to his death; but the stallions bit into his wings harder, and droplets of blood oozed between his feathers. Star shut his mouth and focused on steadying his breathing as he sailed through the pale and chilly afternoon sky. The Blue Mountains rose up in front, framing Valley Field, the home of Sun Herd's closest enemy, Mountain Herd, and its over-stallion, Rockwing.

The steeds flew him up into the mountains and through a dark cloud. The mist blinded him, and the unreasonable fear that they would bump into something gripped him. He sucked in the moist air, choking on it, and his legs galloped for purchase; but he succeeded only in scattering the clouds. The stallions snorted with amusement and dropped toward the forest, their hooves skimming the top branches. Star's gut lurched from the rapid descent, and his damp hide and feathers caused him to shiver. Below he saw three deer hopping through the aspens, avoiding the wide, black shadows of his captors' wings.

After what seemed like a long while, they finally crested a ridge and entered Rockwing's territory. As they swooped over an alpine lake and a meadow thronging with Mountain Herd steeds, Star looked down to see the herd grazing or preening their feathers. A gold dun mare tilted her head skyward as their shadows crossed the sun. She noticed Star and neighed, "It's the black foal of Anok!"

Before the first echo of her cry had faded, the meadow erupted into chaos. Foals stampeded, mares bared their teeth for battle, and warriors took flight, their eyes glowing with a violent mixture of awe and terror. Frostfire and the stallions holding Star landed at the northern edge of the grassy valley. When Star's hooves touched the soil, he was let go.

Star's sore wings collapsed at his sides. Frightened, he turned in a slow circle. Thousands of pegasi faced him, their expressions fierce and their feathers vibrating. The Mountain Herd steeds were short, with wide faces and thick legs like tree trunks.

Star swallowed as fear washed over him. He wished he had not gone into the woods to practice flying alone. At the same time he thought how strange it was that this fierce herd was afraid of him.

The sound of flapping wings made Star turn his head as a brilliant silver Appaloosa with dark blue and gray feathers landed a winglength away. His thick neck was arched and proud as he trotted toward the black foal. "They call you Star?" he asked.

Star shut his mouth, afraid to speak. He knew that unless Thunderwing was prepared to start a war, he couldn't rescue Star from the depths of Rockwing's territory. His fate was in the wings of this unpredictable herd, and Star had not been in this much danger since the day he was born.

"Come with me," said the battle-scarred stallion.

Star hesitated for a moment, and Frostfire shoved him forward. "Follow Rockwing."

They trotted to a clump of white cedars and halted.

"I will make this quick so we can get you back home before you're missed," Rockwing said.

Star blinked rapidly. *They were going to let him go?*

"Thunderwing is going to execute you on your first birthday."

Star said nothing, hoping they hadn't dragged him here just to tell him that.

Rockwing narrowed his eyes. "But you already know that, don't you?"

The patchy clouds drifted, allowing the sun to peek through. Star closed his eyes and let the rays warm him. "Yes," he said simply. He knew he was scheduled to die this winter, but he was still relieved to know he wasn't going to die today.

"I'm offering you a deal that will save your life," Rockwing said.

Star opened his eyes. "What?"

Rockwing continued. "The over-stallions of Anok are afraid of you. I'm not."

Star looked the silver Appaloosa in the face. Rockwing's belligerent eyes were shiny and black, like the hard shells of beetles.

"Do you know *why* they're afraid of you?" Rockwing asked.

Frostfire squeezed Star's wing harder so he would answer immediately. "Because they think I'm the destroyer, not the healer," Star said, grimacing.

Rockwing huffed. "They don't care which one you are. Whether you unite the herds through peace or conquer them through war, they will lose their power. That's what they're afraid of."

Star glared at him. "So why aren't you afraid of me?"

"I want to make a pact with you."

A deep chill settled in his heart. Star shook his head and whispered, "No." Frostfire shoved his wing back so hard, his legs buckled and he saw stars.

"Let him go," said Rockwing.

Frostfire let go, and Star fell, then staggered to his hooves.

"If you join me, I will protect you from the over-stallions of Anok," said Rockwing. "I'll make sure you receive your power from the star, and then we'll unite the herds into one and rule them side by side as dual over-stallions. Everybody wins. No one gets hurt." He leaned into Star, almost touching foreheads with him. "And no one gets executed."

It didn't sound like the worst thing to Star, but his gut roiled. "The other herds won't agree to that. Like you said, they're afraid of losing power."

Rockwing nickered. "You can force them to unite. They don't have to want it."

"But that's not uniting; that's conquering."

Rockwing pinned his ears. "Do you want to save your life, black foal? Thunderwing will kill you, and if he fails, then Icewing will, or Sandwing, or Snakewing. Of the five herds, I'm your only hope."

Star imagined his mother's gentle white face. Light-feather had not migrated with him for hundreds of miles and then died giving birth so that he could repay her by conquering the five herds of Anok. She believed that when he received the fire from the ancient, golden star that appeared over Anok every hundred years, he would be a healer, not a destroyer. And she wasn't the only one who believed it. There were others in Sun Herd who believed it too. Star took a deep breath and shook his head. "No, Rockwing. I won't do it."

Rockwing charged, closing the few feet between them, slicing the forest floor with his sharpened hooves. "You will," he shouted.

Star crouched, ears flat, tail tucked, bearing the wrath of the over-stallion, which washed over him like a hot breeze and yet caused his legs to tremble. They stared at each other for a long time, but Star didn't back down.

Rockwing lashed his tail. "Your herd won't protect you, Star. Come to me when you change your mind. I'll be waiting." He nodded at Frostfire. "Take him away."

Frostfire pushed Star, then led him out of the shade of the trees. The gray and the pinto joined them, and they swept Star up and out of Mountain Herd's territory.

They flew low this time, darting between the oaks in the open plains. And then they dropped Star into Feather Lake and flew away.

2

SECRETS

STAR PLUNKED INTO THE SHALLOW END WITH A loud splash, startling a flock of geese. He trotted out of the lake, shook himself, and collapsed, exhausted, in the coarse sand.

He lay for a long time, swatting flies with his tail and thinking about what had just happened. The Hundred Year Star blazed next to the sun, visible even during the brightest day. It followed him, seeming to stalk him from space, and it grew larger each day. In seven cycles of the moon it would be winter and Star's birthday. At midnight the star would drop low in the sky, transfer its fire to him, and transform him, maybe into a killer—if he lived that long.

"There you are," a voice rang out, its familiar tone lifting his spirits. It was his best friend, Morningleaf. He looked up to see the chestnut filly soar down out of the fir trees, followed by the twin foals, Bumblewind and Echofrost.

They landed next to him, chattering and cheerful. Morningleaf greeted him, blowing softly into his nose. His friends obviously had no idea he'd just been transported into the heart of Mountain Herd and back. Already it felt like a dream.

"We've been looking for you," said Morningleaf.

"Did you see Brackentail and Stripestorm?" Star asked them.

"I saw them," said Bumblewind. "They came running out of the woods like they were being chased by wolves."

"Did they say anything?"

Bumblewind looked at his twin sister. She shrugged her wings. "Not to us. They joined up with the other foals to play."

"Are you okay?" Morningleaf asked, nodding at the cut on Star's shoulder. She rushed to examine it. "Did Brackentail do this to you?" She looked around for the brown colt, her ears pinned.

Star soothed her. "I'm fine. It's just a scratch." But he

couldn't believe Brackentail and Stripestorm hadn't gone for help. Members of his own herd had left him to die. Already he saw that Rockwing's words were true. Heaviness and emptiness rolled through him at the same time.

Morningleaf looked back toward Dawn Meadow, Sun Herd's main grazing land, and scowled. "He's a featherhead, but Star, why were you out here alone? It's not safe."

Star twitched his ears. "I was practicing." He wouldn't tell anyone, including his friends, about Rockwing's offer. His friends would worry, and Sun Herd was already suspicious of him, and they didn't need another reason to fear him.

Star glanced at Morningleaf, feeling unhappy that he couldn't tell her what had just happened. Her dam, Silvercloud, adopted Star after his mother died. Ever since, he and the chestnut filly shared everything. Morningleaf's eyes swept his oversize black wings, dusty from dragging on the ground, his torn feathers hanging off the edges like moss. "Any luck with the flying?" she asked.

Star shook his curly black mane. "No. I can't even lift my wings off my back, let alone flap them."

"Did those colts see you trying to fly?" Morningleaf asked. "Is that how the fight started?"

Star swished his tail as if he could erase the day. "No.

They talked about my mother."

Morningleaf narrowed her eyes. "Don't listen to them. Your mother is a legend."

"I know," Star whispered, nodding his head. Each century when the Hundred Year Star appeared, a black foal was born to one mare in Anok—and this century, that mare had been his dam, Lightfeather.

Morningleaf took a deep, proud breath. "No pregnant mare could have migrated alone, with no help from the herd, like she did. She's incredible."

Star knew all about that, but it didn't make him feel any better, because his mother had died and was gone forever.

Bumblewind trotted to Star and wrapped his wing around his neck. "Anyway, if you keep practicing, you'll fly one day, Star. I know it. Nightwing was born a dud too."

Morningleaf smacked him. "Don't talk about Nightwing."

Star exhaled. Nightwing was a black foal that lived four hundred years ago. The prophecy of the black foal decreed that the Hundred Year Star would transfer its supernatural fire to the colt at midnight on his first birthday. The star would then disappear for another hundred years, and the black foal would become the most powerful pegasus in Anok. But black foals were not regular pegasi to begin with, the most obvious difference being their color. Black coats existed for land horses, but not for pegasi. And their long legs and oversize wings, malformations that caused life-threatening early births, also made them different from the others in their herd. The foals who survived were duds, and most starved to death. But Nightwing had been an exception—his mother had survived.

Since a mare from a different herd was chosen each century to bear the black foal, the herd that received the special colt was known in Anok as the guardian herd. It was the over-stallion's right either to protect or destroy the rare colt, who some pegasi viewed as dangerous and others viewed as extraordinary. This century's guardian herd was Sun Herd, and the over-stallion, Thunderwing, viewed Star as dangerous. Thunderwing didn't believe any one pegasus should wield so much power and vowed to end Star's life on his birthday. He'd sent messengers to all the herds informing them about his decision.

Star shuddered just thinking about his upcoming execution. The fire of the Hundred Year Star terrified the steeds of Anok because it could be used to unite them or destroy them—and no pegasus, not even Star, was sure if he would have any choice in how the power affected him.

All the old stories pictured Nightwing as a polite and friendly foal right up until his first birthday, and then he'd turned on the herds, attacking them, setting their grasslands on fire, and driving them to the edge of extinction. Star's guardian herd feared he would do the same. So the fact that Nightwing had also been born a dud didn't comfort Star.

But Lightfeather had believed Star was good. And because of Lightfeather's belief, Silvercloud, the lead mare of Sun Herd, promised the dying mare she would protect Star as long as she could.

The sounds of his friends nickering reminded Star where he was and that he was soaking wet. He shook himself hard, dousing them in water, and his friends scrambled away, whinnying in delight.

"Well, since we're all here, who wants to play water tag?" asked Echofrost.

"You're it," whinnied Morningleaf, tagging Star.

His friends galloped into the water. Star didn't feel like playing, but he didn't want to return to the herd either, so he chased his three friends into the lake.

He dived under and let the cool water soothe his throbbing wings and raise them off his back. He glided in a lazy circle around Bumblewind, who was not a fast swimmer.

Morningleaf paddled above them, her wings extended and her neck flat, the sunlight filtering through her aqua feathers casting stripes of color across the water. Star floated over the tops of the lake plants. Fat fish and tiny minnows darted out of his path. Down here he could pretend he was a regular flying foal like his friends, a full member of Sun Herd with a proper herd name. He was Starlight the colt, not Star the black foal of Anok, and he could fly—until he ran out of breath.

The four of them played until Star's heavy wings began to cramp again. "I'm done," he said. He crawled out of the flat blue water and then rolled onto his back. The rough sand was hot, and it soothed his muscles. His friends shook themselves dry and picked at the plants along the shoreline, their ears swiveling with each croak of a frog. They were just days away from their weaning, but they still preferred warm, sweet milk to bitter grass.

"I'm hot," said Bumblewind. It was early summer, and the low sun burned their pelts.

Echofrost was preening her feathers. "Let's go back then."

"Come on." Morningleaf chose a narrow, winding path to return to the lower plains where Sun Herd grazed. She broke into a slow trot.

"You three can fly," Star said. "I don't mind."

Morningleaf snorted and kept trotting. "Of course not, we'll walk with you."

The friends rounded a bend and skidded into the dangling hooves of Brackentail, Stripestorm, and a red roan filly named Flamesky, who were flying several feet above the path.

"Look, guys," said Flamesky, "it's a band of horses." The group landed on the dirt path, blocking Star and his friends.

Star locked eyes with Brackentail. The brown colt appeared stunned to see him still alive. Star wondered if Brackentail was returning to Feather Lake hoping to find that the four Mountain Herd stallions had killed him.

Morningleaf pinned her ears. "Let us pass."

Brackentail huffed and spread his wings. "Why don't you fly over us?" He looked pointedly at Star.

Morningleaf whirled around and kicked Brackentail in the chest, knocking him out of the sky. The colt slammed into the ground, wheezing and coughing. Flamesky lunged at Morningleaf but pulled herself back just as fast. Morningleaf was the daughter of Sun Herd's over-stallion, Thunderwing, and Flamesky was better off not harassing her. Brackentail's friends looked at each other, unsure how to proceed.

Morningleaf took advantage of their uncertainty and pushed past them. "Just ignore them," she said to Star, Echofrost, and Bumblewind. They followed her past the foals.

Brackentail regained his breath and flapped into the sky. "You better watch yourself, Morningleaf," he threatened from the safety of the heights. "Hanging around the black foal is making you sour." Brackentail's entire body quivered as he said the words, and then he and his friends flew away before Morningleaf could respond to them.

"Don't listen to that nonsense," said Bumblewind.

"I'm not," said Morningleaf, her feathers rattling with fury.

But Star heard it, and wondered why Brackentail cared so much about Morningleaf. The big colt was never anything but mean to her.

The four friends finished their journey home in silence. Eventually the sloping path led them out of the trees and revealed the lower plain. Four thousand Sun Herd pegasi grazed in the green valley, their glossy feathers shimmering as they fanned themselves. Compact foals darted between tufts of grass like hummingbirds, their agile wings short and bright. Captains drilled their platoons in the foothills to the west, and fragrant summer flowers dotted the grassland.

Star paused, surveying the impressive sight of his herd. "Let's look for a moment."

Bumblewind gave a hearty sigh and pawed the ground. "I'm hungry."

"Just for a moment," Star promised. He enjoyed watching sunsets, pretty birds, rainbows, cloud formations—whatever caught his eye, but his friends had little patience for those things.

He looked to the left toward the edge of the forest where his mother's grave was, a mound of rocks piled inside a circle of tall redwood trees. He'd only spent a few hours with Lightfeather before she'd died. He could still remember how the glow from the Hundred Year Star had made her white body look gold. While Sun Herd had argued to destroy him immediately, she'd ignored their threats and whispered secrets into Star's ears until he fell asleep. Then she'd died with him curled between her front legs. He'd been too young to understand the words she'd spoken, but he knew they resided in him all the same, engraved deep in his memory.

Lightfeather was a legend to some Sun Herd pegasi and an unlucky orphan to others. She'd been born to Snow

Herd in the far north, the illegitimate foal of Icewing. But the lead mare there had driven Lightfeather and her mother out when she was just a filly. A Sun Herd patrol had found Lightfeather hiding in a tree a few days later. A bear had killed and eaten her mother, so she was alone. They'd brought her to Sun Herd's territory, where Silvercloud took pity on her and adopted her. When the filly grew up and became pregnant with the black foal, many pegasi in Sun Herd wished Silvercloud had left Lightfeather to die in the woods. Lightfeather became an outsider, just like her colt was now.

"I'm really hungry," Bumblewind said again, groaning.

The words pulled Star from his reverie. "All right. Let's go."

They continued their descent and separated when they reached the long grass in the field.

"There's Mother," said Echofrost. She and her brother kicked off and flew to Crystalfeather to nurse. The chestnut mare welcomed her foals with an anxious whinny.

Star and Morningleaf trotted to Silvercloud's side. She nuzzled them and then noticed Star's wound. "Star, what happened to your shoulder?"

"He fell," said Morningleaf, covering the truth.

Star was grateful for her quick response because

Morningleaf knew he didn't like Silvercloud to worry about him. But Silvercloud was lead mare of Sun Herd and responsible for the safety of all the foals. She was not so easily fooled. "Fell, huh?" she asked, pricking her ears.

"I was trying to fly," said Star.

The gray mare nodded. "Would you like Sweetroot to take a look at it? She may have some medicine to heal it."

"No. It's fine." Sweetroot was Sun Herd's medicine mare, and Star saw her often enough as it was. Each morning she rubbed a mixture of marigold and comfrey across the torn ends of his wings.

Silvercloud nodded and returned to grazing. She nickered with contentment as Star nursed from the ground and Morningleaf nursed from the air, her rapid wingbeats a blur of aqua as she shoved her nose into Silvercloud's side. When they'd drunk their fill, the two foals collapsed on a blanket of dandelions.

As Star closed his eyes, dark thoughts entered his mind, and within minutes of falling asleep, a nightmare gripped him.

He was a newborn foal visiting the fresh grave of his mother when a black shadow suddenly blotted out the sun. Star raised his head and saw Thunderwing flying to Lightfeather's grave with his captains in tow. Silvercloud, who was standing next to Star, inched closer as the stallions landed and folded their wings. Star noticed that even the daylight was tinged by the gold fire of the Hundred Year Star, and it was under this light that Star met the crimson-feathered over-stallion for the first time.

Thunderwing stared into Star's eyes, and Silvercloud flared her wings protectively.

"He'll never fly," Thunderwing said, directing his comment to Silvercloud.

The mare said nothing.

Thunderwing spread his wings to their full length and reared, towering over Star, who was only hours old. He lunged forward, slamming the ground with his front hooves, and the force of the blow rattled Star's teeth. "If you survive," he said, leaning toward Star, eye to eye with him, "you will not live past a year, for I will execute you on your first birthday. I won't let you threaten the five herds of Anok."

Thunderwing lashed his tail and addressed the fresh grave. "Fly straight and find your rest, Lightfeather." He turned and flew away into the bright gold light of the Hundred Year Star, his bloodred feathers floating in his wake.

3

CHASE

"LET'S PRETEND WE'RE DESERT HERD STEEDS ON A high flight," said Morningleaf, opening her wings. It was several days after his kidnapping, and Star was playing with his friends at the eastern end of Dawn Meadow.

"We're not allowed to fly higher than the trees until we're weaned," Bumblewind reminded her, chewing on a blade of grass.

"We're not really going to fly," said Morningleaf, with a casual glance at Star. "But let's pretend we're on a high flight to where the blue sky turns black."

"You know Desert Herd steeds can't fly that high," said Echofrost.

Morningleaf flicked her small, curved ears. "Yes, they

can. Raincloud did it four hundred years ago."

"That's a legend." Echofrost lashed her tail at a fly crawling up her leg. "Legends aren't real; they're exaggerated. Everyone knows that."

"Can we just play?" asked Morningleaf. She flapped her wings and galloped across the grass. Echofrost followed. Star watched as the fillies flattened their necks and angled their wings as if they were really flying.

He whinnied and joined them, catching and passing them easily. The nice thing about his long legs was that he was fast—faster than any of the foals in Sun Herd. Star whipped around and faced Morningleaf, cutting her off. She dodged him, stubbing her hoof, and tumbled across the grass, nickering happily.

Morningleaf sat up and shook a flower petal off her head. "You two will be Snow Herd raiders," she said, pointing her wing at Star and Bumblewind. "Try to catch us. Come on, Echofrost."

Echofrost cantered up beside Morningleaf, flicking Star with her white tail.

"Hey!" he nickered and chased her, Bumblewind galloping beside him.

"Notice how they made us Snow Herd steeds, the worst fliers in Anok," Bumblewind huffed. "So if we catch them, they'll say we're cheating."

"But we're bigger and stronger," Star said, running faster, his heart thrumming in his chest. He felt like a regular pegasus colt when he played with his friends, like he belonged.

The foals galloped across the field, wings flapping except for Star's. Morningleaf took flight up and over the growing grass with Echofrost flying beside her, staying just a short winglength over the colts' heads. "Pretend we're higher than the clouds," Morningleaf said to Echofrost, her eyes gleaming.

Bumblewind grabbed his twin sister's tail and pulled her lower. "You're captured," he said, imitating the deep, rumbling neigh of a stallion.

Star reared, snatching Morningleaf's tail and landing her. "You're both Snow Herd fillies now," he said.

Morningleaf squealed and struggled to escape his grasp. Star pinned her against a tall oak tree. "You'll never escape me, red filly," he said, trying to sound serious while she pretended to be afraid.

"Can we play?" said a voice, interrupting the fun. Star looked over and saw Brackentail and the other Sun Herd foals.

Star flattened his ears, and Brackentail glared at him,

lashing his tail. The brown colt seemed to feel no guilt about abandoning Star at Feather Lake.

Morningleaf's ribs expanded in a deep breath, and Star realized he was crushing her. He released her so she could answer. "Sure," she said.

"What are we playing?" asked a little dappled filly.

Morningleaf looked embarrassed. "Just chase."

The filly brightened. "Sounds fun." She darted forward, and all the foals scattered, flying after one another, their hooves skimming the grass.

Star bolted with an excited whinny and sped into the woods as fast as he could, determined to outrun anyone chasing him. After a while he glanced back to see who was coming after him, but no one was there. His legs were longer than the others foals' legs; maybe he was too fast for them. He slowed, breathing hard, ready to dash away at the first sign of a foal.

He circled the trees for a long time, flicking his ears and listening for any movement. But slowly the truth hit him like a tail smacking an oblivious fly—no one had chased him. The thrill of the chase melted away, and he noticed his back muscles were throbbing from dragging his long wings.

In the distance he heard abrupt nickers and squeals

as the foals called to one another.

"I found you."

"You're it."

"Try and catch me."

He felt silly standing in a thicket, panting and waiting for a chaser who would never come, but he couldn't go back so soon, alone. They would understand what had happened, and Brackentail would make fun of him. Defeated, Star lay down with a sigh and munched on nearby huckleberries. He glanced at the dark forest around him, and his ears slumped. His eyesight was his sharpest sense, but in this thick forest, the shrubs and branches blocked his vision.

Suddenly, he heard a twig snap, loud and sharp—ominous—as though something heavy had stepped on it. Frightened, he knew he had to get back to the herd. He would trot home another way so no one would notice him returning by himself. He got up and made his way through the trees. He found a deer trail and followed it, trying to be quiet by placing each hoof softly in front of the other. After a while he emerged from the forest on a high ridge overlooking Dawn Meadow. Spread below him was Sun Herd, grazing, their wings blinking open and closed. The sun was setting, casting orange light across their vibrant feathers, and as usual, the pegasi had gathered into their family groups for the evening.

Above him, Thunderwing's sky patrols circled, keeping an eye out for predators and raiding parties from other herds. The birds had ceased their singing, and the crickets began theirs. The herd was peaceful right now, a unit that worked together for the safety of everyone—except for him, the black foal. Only Silvercloud had sworn to protect him, partly because she was the lead mare and it was her duty, but mostly because she had promised his dam, and Lightfeather had believed that Star was good. Right now Silvercloud was standing alone under a tree.

"There you are," said a voice, startling him.

He looked down and saw Morningleaf climbing the ridge, digging her hooves into the sharp rocks and wincing. "Why aren't you flying?" he asked, perplexed.

Her eyes widened in surprise, and she huffed. "I don't know. Habit, I guess."

Star sighed. "That's my fault."

Morningleaf reached the top of the ridge and stood beside him. "Don't talk like that."

"It's true."

She flicked her ears and looked out over the herd. "I'm

going to be a lead mare someday," she said, ignoring his comment.

"Why?"

She blinked at him. "Why not?"

Star tossed his thick mane. Morningleaf was born to lead and protect, but the job wasn't without its dangers. Lead mares were responsible for leading migrations and for the safety of all the mares and foals. If anything went wrong—if her charges were kidnapped, killed by predators, lost on migration, or harmed in any way—the lead mare could be punished, and the punishments were severe; but nothing Star could say about it would change Morningleaf's mind.

He nickered softly. "We should join your mother. She's all by herself."

Morningleaf fluffed her feathers and snorted. "That's my father's fault."

They proceeded down the ridge toward the herd. Star watched Thunderwing land from a flight and canter away from Silvercloud toward a group of single stallions. He spent every evening with them and none with Silvercloud. Star knew Thunderwing was angry with his mate for asserting her protection over Star. She'd forced him to choose between her and the black foal, at least until his birthday, and he'd agreed, but he'd also come to regret it. The breakup of Morningleaf's family was because of Star, and it made him feel terrible.

"Why were you up there by yourself anyway?" asked Morningleaf as they descended into Dawn Meadow.

Star gazed into her amber-colored eyes, so bright and alive, and he wondered what her life would be like if he weren't in it. She'd have both her parents. She'd have more friends. She'd get to fly more often. He pricked his ears, unwilling to tell her the truth about his humiliation in the forest. It would only upset her, so he said, "I was looking at the sunset."

Morningleaf nickered, curious. "The sunset? Why?"

Star arched his neck. "Why not?"

Morningleaf snorted and took off across the meadow at a gallop. "Catch me if you can!" she whinnied over her shoulder.

Star leaped after her, his heart light, and he was grateful. He didn't have a lot of friends in Sun Herd, but the friends he had were the best.

4

WEANLINGS

"LOOK AT THE CLOUDS," SAID ECHOFROST. IT WAS several days later. Star and his friends were resting in the tall summer grass. The clouds were scattered above them across a dazzling blue sky. They appeared flat and gray on the bottom, but erupted into tall, fluffy, drifting shapes. Star's thoughts floated with them—the weaning was today, and the migration was tomorrow.

"I'm going to fly through those clouds on the migration," said Echofrost, her sleek silver body glistening in the sun. "They look soft."

"They're wet," said Morningleaf. "When my mother lands after a flight, she's damp. She calls it 'cloud sweat.'"

Echofrost exhaled. "I don't care; I want to see them up close."

The sky was the only view that ignited the imaginations of Star's friends. The highest they had flown so far was a few winglengths above the grass.

Since Star couldn't fly, he'd be migrating by hoof with the walkers. "How will they wean us?" he asked, changing the subject.

Bumblewind twitched his ears. "I bet there will be a ceremony and a speech."

Morningleaf nodded. "And maybe a cloud flight to celebrate."

Echofrost stared across the meadow at her mother. "I don't want to wean."

"Don't think about what you're losing, think about what you're gaining," said Morningleaf. "We'll finally get to fly higher than the trees, and besides, the herd can't migrate with nursing foals." She had their weanling lives all planned out, but Star and the others wanted to enjoy their last day as foals.

"All this talk is making me hungry," nickered Bumblewind.

The foals rose and trotted to their respective dams. Silvercloud greeted Star and Morningleaf with a curt nicker. When they nosed into her, she swung her hips out of their reach and kept grazing.

"Mama," Morningleaf said, "we're hungry."

Silvercloud snorted and ripped up a full mouthful of grass. Her lower jaw worked in circles as she chewed. She met their eyes, but her expression was unreadable. Morningleaf shoved her nose into Silvercloud's underbelly, causing her mother to rear and fly away.

Star saw the dams all over the meadow doing the same thing to their foals. "Something is wrong with the mares," he said.

Silvercloud flew a loop over their heads. "It's not us," she nickered, "it's you. You're weaned." She flew away to join the other giddy mares.

"What do you mean? That's it?" cried Morningleaf.

"That's it!" whinnied Silvercloud over her shoulder.

Star and Morningleaf stood on the ground in a daze. They trotted to Echofrost and Bumblewind, who were equally stunned. "I guess there won't be a speech," said Bumblewind.

The four friends stood in the grass and stared at one another, and then the truth dawned. "We're weanlings now," said Star.

Morningleaf flexed her wings and whinnied. "Big,

fluffy clouds—here I come!" She galloped forward, flapping madly, and rose higher than the trees. Echofrost and Bumblewind chased after her, whinnying with delight as they darted through their first cloud.

Star could hear their excited neighs from the ground.

"It *is* wet!" said Echofrost, diving through the clouds.

"I can't see," cried Bumblewind, and then he exploded out of the white mist.

"Everything looks so tiny," neighed Morningleaf, looking down.

Star watched them play, happy for them but with a huge lump in his throat at being left behind. Other foals realized their new freedom and joined his friends in the sky, bombarding through cloud puffs, flying circles around their mothers, and neighing with joy. The dams landed back in the meadow, where they could have the peace and quiet they wanted.

Star tensed when a massive black shadow suddenly swept over the herd. He was relieved to see that it was only Thunderwing, swooping across the sun. Always in the back of his mind, Star worried that Rockwing's stallions would come for him again. He could still feel their sharp teeth marks in his wings.

Thunderwing landed and called Sun Herd to order

with a forceful braying. The foals quickly landed, and the pegasi gathered around, waiting for him to speak.

A hush fell over Sun Herd. "The migration begins tomorrow," he neighed.

Star heard the unique buzzing sound of thousands of pegasi wings vibrating at the same time. Any opportunity to fly long distances was always met with great excitement by his herd. Star's shoulders twitched in response as he tried to lift his wings, longing to rattle his feathers with Sun Herd.

Thunderwing continued his announcement. "The walkers and the dud will leave for the northern meadows at sunrise."

Star ducked his head as many pairs of eyes darted his way. He hated the term "dud" and wished they'd just call him a walker.

Thunderwing flapped his wings and hovered above Sun Herd, dropping bloodred feathers on the grass. "The fliers will follow about a half moon cycle later," he added, "give or take a few days. We should arrive in our northern territory at the same time. Jetfire will give the migration report."

Thunderwing landed, and the cream-colored captain, Jetfire, flew off the grass so all the pegasi could see him.

"We won't have a tailwind like we had last year," he said. "The wind currents are traveling west, toward the ocean. It shouldn't slow us down much if we modify our V formations to accommodate it. I'll set up formation trainings for the seven days before we leave." Jetfire made eye contact with Grasswing, an old, disabled pegasus who could no longer fly. "As for the walkers, the land is dry from drought. Predators will be scarce, but the chance of fires will be high. Keep your noses to the wind and avoid heavy forests."

Morningleaf sidled close to Star. "Fires? That doesn't sound good."

Star preened a hunk of mud out of her flaxen mane. "You worry too much. Anyway, you didn't listen to the good part—scarce predators."

"I heard it," she snorted, unsatisfied. "I'd feel better if I could go with you."

Star stretched to his full height. "I'm the future stallion here; I should be protecting you."

Morningleaf glanced up at him, her ears pricked forward. "Well, there won't be any protecting going on if we aren't together!"

Star nickered. "That's true." He'd never been apart from Morningleaf for more than a few hours. He was going to miss his best friend on his long migration by hoof. It would take his group a full cycle of the moon to migrate. It would take the fliers fewer than ten days.

Jetfire finished his report with ominous news. "Our scouts tell us Mountain Herd will be migrating at the same time as we are."

Echofrost sucked in her breath. "They always leave a moon later. I wonder what changed?"

Star knew what changed. Rockwing wanted to keep track of him.

"We don't expect an interaction with Mountain Herd based on our course of flight and their standard course from years past; but to be safe, we're sending the captain Twistfire to join the walking herd, and Thunderwing and the army will lead the fliers this year, not the lead mare, Silvercloud."

Morningleaf lashed her tail angrily, and she and Star glanced at Silvercloud. The gray mare was expressionless, but Star could tell by the twitching of her ears that she was furious.

"He didn't have to do that," whispered Morningleaf. "Armies lead battles, not migrations. They won't be scouting for watering holes or our favorite traveling foods—they'll just plop us down in the middle of anywhere and call it good, probably fly us too hard too."

Star was surprised to see her so upset, but he didn't believe it was about the watering holes or the rest stops. Taking the migration from Silvercloud was an insult that would be hard for any lead mare, or her filly, to overlook.

Thunderwing dismissed the herd and took flight, soaring toward Feather Lake, followed by Jetfire and a battalion of soldiers.

"Where is Thunderwing going?" Star asked.

"To check our eastern border," said Morningleaf. "Silvercloud saw a Mountain Herd patrol flying there yesterday."

Star shuddered, wondering if the patrol had been looking for him.

"They've been coming too close lately," said Bumblewind.

Morningleaf fluffed her aqua feathers. "Mother says they're outgrowing their territory, and they can't expand because they're surrounded on all sides by the other herds. If disease or famine doesn't reduce their numbers, they're going to have to challenge a herd for more space."

"And we have the best grazing lands in Anok," said Bumblewind, eyes wide.

Morningleaf huffed. "I wouldn't worry; our army is larger."

Echofrost shuddered. "I hear their raiders like to kidnap foals. They keep the fillies and murder the colts."

Morningleaf stamped her hoof. "Stop this talk. A foal has not been taken since my father became over-stallion. The steeds my mother saw were probably just hunting birds' eggs."

Echofrost made a face, pulling back her lips. "That's disgusting."

Morningleaf nodded. "Silvercloud told me they crack the eggs in their teeth and swallow the yellow slime."

Bumblewind gagged. "I knew they were short, hairy, and mean, but I didn't know they ate birds' eggs."

Morningleaf swished her tail. "Forget them. We're weanlings now; let's act like it. We should graze."

"Not me," said Star. "I need to talk to Grasswing about the migration." Grasswing had once been a captain in Thunderwing's army, but after a horrible battle had left him crippled, Thunderwing made him an honorary over-stallion in charge of the Sun Herd walkers: the pegasi who were too old or injured to fly. The walkers were grateful because it was impossible for Thunderwing to protect a herd on the ground and one in the sky at the same time—and Grasswing was a legendary battle steed.

"I still wish I could migrate with you," Morningleaf said to Star. "I like walking."

Star tossed his thick mane. "Thunderwing would never allow it. Flying is safer. There are no fires in the sky, and no bears, pumas, or wolves either."

"You're right about that," she agreed. "But that's not why he said no. I asked him last night, and he said he wouldn't have me traveling on the ground like a common horse." She gave Star a sorrowful look. "Sorry."

Star tried to shrug his wings, and a splitting pain ran down his shoulder blades. "It's okay. I don't want you walking either, so it's settled."

"Want to practice flying again later? I'll help you," Morningleaf offered.

"Sure," said Star. He was currently in the grasp of a horrible wing cramp, but he'd learned to hide this pain from his friends.

"Let's find Grasswing," said Bumblewind.

Star trotted across the field with his friends hovering around him like bees over a flower. Sharp weeds ripped at his feathers, leaving a trail of bright-red blood droplets in his wake. He found Grasswing dozing under a shady oak.

"I've been expecting you," said the old palomino

stallion, opening his eyes as he heard them approach.

"Yes, sir," neighed Star with a bow of his head.

"And I've been watching you. You're fast, but those things get in your way." Grasswing nodded at Star's limp wings.

"Yes, sir," said Star, looking at the ground.

"Can you lift them?"

"No, sir." Star's wings were a sorry sight, he knew. The end feathers were raw and covered in dust. He'd grown used to their weight and the ache they caused, but he was always hot. While the rest of the Sun Herd steeds used their wings to cool their bodies, Star's lay on him like thick moss. He was grateful they were heading north for the summer where it would be cooler.

Grasswing nodded. "All right, son, do your best." He held Star's eyes in his gaze like he was searching his thoughts. "And don't worry; I'll watch out for you during the migration."

Star blinked at him, astonished. The palomino was Thunderwing's oldest friend. His support was powerful. Star took a deep breath and exhaled long and slow; maybe he wasn't as alone as he thought. "Thank you."

Grasswing winked. "We leave tomorrow." With that, the old warrior closed his eyes and returned to dozing.

That evening the newly weaned foals slept away from their dams. It was part punishment, part sorrow, but the mares didn't look punished. They looked relieved. Crystalfeather and Silvercloud had been pulling extra duty nursing doubles, and Star saw them rolling luxuriously on their backs, chatting.

When his friends were asleep, he quietly loped to Lightfeather's grave in the circle of redwood trees. He plucked a pink flower and laid it on the stones that covered her. "I'm leaving tomorrow, Mama," he whispered.

Crickets answered him, and Star felt hollow. He knew the story of his birth: how brave his mother had been, how she massaged him to life when he was born without a heartbeat, how she whispered secrets into his ears until he fell asleep, and how she bled to death in silence.

Tears rolled down his wide cheeks and dropped to the ground. Where the tears fell, the soil shifted, and white flowers sprang from the dirt. This was another, less obvious, sign that he was different from regular pegasi: his tears grew flowers. Normally he stomped them out, embarrassed, but tonight he left them. He liked knowing their roots were growing into the soil around Lightfeather. After a while, Star turned and trotted back to his friends.

5

MIGRATION

THE NEXT MORNING, STAR, GRASSWING, AND THE other walkers gathered under a clump of shady oak trees at dawn. Star was the last to arrive because he was in no hurry to get to the northern territory. He would turn one year old there, and his destiny would be fulfilled, for better or for worse.

Silvercloud trotted to his side followed by Morningleaf, Echofrost, and Bumblewind. "Be safe and listen to Grasswing," Silvercloud said to him.

"I will." Star threw his friends a quick glance. Morningleaf's lip was quivering, and Echofrost and Bumblewind were pacing frantically, either from stress or nursing withdrawals, he wasn't sure. "I'll see you all there," Star said, trying to cheer them.

He looked at Morningleaf. Her light-brown eyes reflected the sky above where she would soon be flying. "Before you know it, we'll be together again," he said. She shoved her muzzle into the crook of his neck and nickered softly. Star longed to join her and the fliers. He wanted to watch the land whiz by under his hooves, to feel the dampness of the clouds, and to see new places. And he didn't want to leave his friends.

Star shook off his thoughts and stepped away from Morningleaf. "Fly safe," he said to all of them, and then he trotted away before he lost control and cried in front of the entire herd.

Without ceremony, Grasswing began the journey north followed by about a hundred walkers. When pegasi migrated by air, they flew in organized V formations, like geese. The bigger steeds took turns bearing the brunt of the headwinds while the smaller ones drafted in their wakes. But when pegasi traveled on the ground, they lacked such organization. Star fell into the rear of the herd and noticed that the walkers traveled like sullen refugees—together but alone—as if the only thing they had in common was that they were walking in the same direction.

A cloud of dust quickly formed as they headed north and left Sun Herd behind. Star coughed and snorted, trying to clear his nose and throat. He'd seen land horses once, drinking at Feather Lake. They were graceful when they traveled, born to run, but he thought the pegasi tried too hard. They walked with heads high because they were used to seeing the ground from the heights, and they fiddled with their wings, trying to find a flying rhythm that matched a walking gait.

Since Star had never flown, he picked up on the secret to ground walking pretty fast. It was simple; one just had to relax. Grasswing knew the secret too. He sauntered forward, head low and bobbing, wings tucked, hooves lazy. In spite of the horrible dust, Star remained at the back of the herd. He was used to being alone.

For half a moon they walked without incident. Grasswing led them over open vistas and through towering redwood forests. They drank from sky-blue lakes and crossed meadows dotted with colorful flowers and white butterflies, and they slept each night under a clear and glittering sky. The beauty distracted Star from the painful sag of his wings. The few predators they encountered moved out of their way, content to mind their own business.

Star often found himself walking behind Mossberry, an old mare who entertained him with stories. She was ninety-two and the oldest pegasus in Sun Herd. Her back swayed, the tops of her haunches were hollow, and her ribs showed, but her dark eyes were warm and bright.

Star followed her now, letting her swishing tail hypnotize him as the herd traveled through a large strip of open land between two dense forests. As usual, they walked due north toward the cooler section of their territory. Green grass would be plentiful there even in the late summer and fall, when their southern lands were dry. The sun's heat was mild on his black coat, and he was content.

Then suddenly, out of nowhere, he felt the ground vibrate under his hooves. He pricked his ears, listening and slowing his gait, as the strange vibrations grew stronger. Puzzled, Star craned his neck as high as he could and looked around. He saw nothing unusual. Mossberry nickered. "Stay close, Star."

Grasswing pranced through the herd of walkers, his tail high and twisted. He scanned the horizon.

Star heard something that sounded like heavy rain. Out of the darkening sky, white flakes drifted with the breeze. Snow? Star stuck out his tongue and caught a flake. He'd never seen snow, but Silvercloud's stories described it as frozen water. This was dry and tasted like dirt.

But the flakes didn't explain the approaching noise. Star swiveled his ears and finally placed the sound: hoofbeats. Mossberry straggled to a halt on stiff legs. The walking herd flapped their useless wings, and their shrill whinnies erased the last of Star's contentment. Something was very wrong.

The thundering of the hooves grew louder, and Star saw distant trees swaying in the wake of the noise. He trotted to Mossberry's side like an anxious foal and stared at the forest from which the sound was coming. "What is it?"

"I don't know," she whinnied, and reared suddenly as a herd of land horses exploded out of the brush. "Move," she screamed, knocking Star clear of their path.

Star bleated, neighing to Mossberry over the ringing hoofbeats. "What's happening?"

The horses raced past them, jumping fallen logs and short bushes, stumbling, and careening—a blur of legs and terror.

The Sun Herd walkers clumped together in the open space between the two forests, watching the stampede. Star's nerves tingled, and his breath came fast, like he was running too. If the land horses noticed them, Star couldn't tell. They galloped thoughtlessly, gripped and propelled by their fright. He reared to get a better view over the backs of the adults. The horses were built to run. They leaped with grace, landed without missing a beat, unburdened by useless wings. They were plain, mostly brown, but long legged and refined. Being called a horse wasn't the worst thing, he decided.

Then horribly and suddenly, Star smelled the source of their fear just as Grasswing's alarm pealed through the valley. "Fire!"

The pegasi whirled and immediately chased after the horses. Their compact bodies were built to fly, not run, and most had never jumped. Star's herd dodged fallen trees and thick bushes that the land horses jumped with ease, and it slowed their escape. The fire roared out of the brush, dropped to the low grass, and chased them with insatiable fury.

In the chaos, Star lost sight of Mossberry. His long legs carried him past larger pegasi as the herd thundered through the valley toward the woods. Deer bounded past Star, and their hooves flushed jackrabbits out of the grass ahead of him. Some of the hares were trampled as they zigzagged through the maze of hooves.

Star was almost to the forest when he heard a horrific

shriek. He turned his head and saw a wing-shaped burst of flames behind him. "Mossberry!" he whinnied, digging in his hooves and turning back. Grasswing, who was behind him, did the same.

Popping sparks had landed on Mossberry's dry feathers. She flapped her wings, but the air she created fed the flames. Her magenta feathers curled and turned black.

"Help me!" she screamed, rearing up, her eyes rounded and white rimmed.

"I'm coming!" Star cried, neighing for help and cantering toward her.

Grasswing blocked him. "No, Star!"

Mossberry's flesh and feathers melted off her wings, and Star saw the outline of her thin bones. She dropped to the ground, engulfed in flames, her legs flailing upside down.

"I need to help her!" Star screeched, pushing hard against Grasswing.

The stallion shoved him toward the woods. "No! Run, Star!"

The fire finished with Mossberry and blazed toward them. The smell of smoke awakened something in Star he couldn't control, and he turned and fled.

As the pegasi herd crashed into the forest, the trees

split their paths. Star ran away from the smoke and fire, following the trampled tracks of the horses, his lungs burning as he coughed from the smoke. When the fire reached the forest it slowed, toppling trees and swallowing them whole. The stampeding horses, deer, and pegasi raced ahead of the flames, through the brush and trees, and exited the forest on the other side. The deer scattered, the horses veered south, and the pegasi turned north. Grasswing whistled a call to gather the walkers quickly. Star ran to his side with a few dozen others.

By evening the entire herd was reunited on a large meadow. They rested and caught their breath. They were dazed and thirsty as Grasswing counted them. Only Mossberry was missing. There was no need for Grasswing to explain her absence; news of her horrific death had spread quickly through the herd.

He gathered the walkers for a brief burial ceremony, though there was no body for them to cover with stones. "Who will speak for Mossberry?"

A mare, well into her sixties, lifted her head. "Mossberry, filly of Windheart, you told the best stories in Sun Herd."

Several elders nickered, but their expressions were downcast.

"You're in the golden meadow now. Fly straight and find your rest." The mare closed her eyes.

"Will anyone else speak for Mossberry?" Grasswing asked.

Twistfire stepped forward. "The last pegasus she spoke to was Star."

Star stiffened at the mention of his name, and the herd rustled.

Grasswing interrupted. "If no one else will speak for Mossberry, we need to find water and rest."

Twistfire galloped forward and wrapped his muscled wing around Star's neck. Star gasped and tried to pull away. "He's bad luck." Twistfire looked at each steed. "He was the last one to speak to Mossberry before she died."

The walkers fluttered their wings, whispering.

"Let him go," said Grasswing. The palomino thrust his chest and pranced, ready for battle. The walkers, mostly elders, crowded close to him, glaring at Twistfire.

Twistfire grumbled and released Star. "Mossberry's blood is on your wings, black foal."

"That's enough." Grasswing pulled Star away from him. "There's a river nearby," he said to the herd. Then, turning to Star, he whispered, "Keep close to me."

Star followed just behind the old warrior. When they were some distance ahead of the rest, Grasswing spoke. "Don't listen to Twistfire."

Star avoided his gaze; his belly was a coil of nerves and grief.

"I mean it, son. Don't let him tell you who you are."

Star lifted his chin. "The legends say who I am, Grasswing. And pegasi aren't safe around me. Twistfire's right. I'm not lucky."

Grasswing snorted. "Quite the opposite. It's Mossberry who wasn't lucky. Don't let the herd blame you for their troubles, Star. That fire had nothing to do with you. I've lived seventy-two seasons, and there have been fires and bears, wars and raids, murders and kidnappings my whole life." He sighed. "As far as I can tell, nothing's changed since you came along. If you're a curse, then I can just add you to the long list of curses that plague the pegasi. If you're the healer—well then, maybe you'll change the world. We have nothing to lose for gaining you, Star. Tell me something: Who tried to help Mossberry while the rest of them ran faster?" He swept his wing to indicate the entire herd of walkers.

Star shuffled his hooves. "I did, but I was afraid."

Grasswing snorted. "We're all afraid, but you didn't run away. Seems to me you're on the right track." Grasswing patted Star on the back and looked ahead. "Ah, there it is," he said, "the river."

Star and the rest of the herd approached the river's edge and dunked their muzzles into the cold water, soothing their parched throats. The sun was setting, and Grasswing signaled that they would rest until morning.

Star settled down for the night alone. Images of Mossberry's burning body rattled him every time he closed his eyes. He missed his friends and longed to talk to Morningleaf, to tell her what had happened. He preened his smoky feathers and thought of the horses running from the fire. As much as his wings irritated him, he didn't really want them removed. He wanted to fly, and the urge was expanding in him every day.

Flight lessons would start for his friends when they became yearlings. Star would give anything to go to flight school with them, but he knew his time would be cut short on his birthday.

Or he could accept Rockwing's deal.

Star sighed. Maybe the Hundred Year Star would let him go. It was clear he wasn't the stuff of legends; he couldn't tuck his wings on his back, let alone rule the five herds of Anok. The legends, like his wings, were a cruel joke. They promised freedom but delivered only pain.

Star fell asleep and dreamed he lived in the clouds—high above forest fires and angry bears—where pegasi flew without fear.

6

SKY MEADOW

THE REST OF THE MIGRATION TO SUN HERD'S northern territory passed slowly and without incident. On the final day, Star woke from a terrible dream. He was out of breath and covered in leaves, like he'd been rolling.

"You okay there, Star?" asked Grasswing, stretching his wings in the dawn light.

Star stood up and shook off the loose leaves stuck to his mane and tail. Above him the Hundred Year Star rested low in the sky. He'd been dreaming about the starfire that would invade his body at midnight on his birthday, if he were still alive. He dreamed the power would change him into a destroyer, like it did Nightwing. Thinking about it now, a tear formed in his eye and rolled down his cheek.

In the dream he attacked Sun Herd and accidentally set Morningleaf on fire. Just before he woke, he watched Morningleaf's aqua feathers melt off her bones, like Mossberry's had. Star shuddered. He couldn't tell Grasswing this, so he said, "I'm fine, just tired of walking."

Grasswing nodded skeptically but said, "Well, I have good news for you. We'll be home today."

"Today?" Star was overjoyed. He would see his friends.

A few hours later, Star and Grasswing emerged from the dense sycamore forest into the open plains. Lush long grass, teeming with life, was spread for miles ahead of them. Huge, puffy clouds floated across a deep-blue sky, thick trees rose from the ground like giants, and a creek bubbled steadily nearby. "Is this the northern territory?" Star asked, awed.

"It is." Grasswing flared his nostrils and trumpeted news of their arrival. His voice, strong and clear, carried for miles, and it wasn't the first time Star could see the remnants of the legendary warrior he'd once been.

Star stepped into the northern lands, exhausted. His legs trembled as he set each hoof down. The fire had forced Grasswing to change course, and they'd had to take a roundabout way home, adding many days to their journey. And the new path didn't take them past any lakes, so the

Sun Herd walkers had been unable to bathe. Star's hide was stained with mud and infested with burrs, and he still smelled like smoke.

But his heart lifted when a large formation of Sun Herd fliers came into view, coasting down from a plateau and landing in front of the walkers.

"Where's Star?" he heard someone say.

He raised his neck but didn't see any of his friends.

"Star!" Morningleaf cried as she shoved through the herd and barreled into him, burrowing her nose into his thick black mane. "You're home."

Star exhaled as though he'd been holding his breath for an entire moon and nickered softly. "Yes. I'm home." He looked up as Echofrost and Bumblewind galloped to his side. "You're all here," Star said. "All safe."

"Of course," said Morningleaf. "It was you we were worried about!"

"We heard about . . . the fire," said Bumblewind, glancing at Star's singed feathers. "Are you hurt?"

Star kicked the dirt, his throat too tight to speak right away. After a moment he murmured, "I'm fine."

Morningleaf looked up at him, her eyes bright and curious, taking in his condition. Star could only imagine how he looked to her: thin and wiry, with shredded wing tips and a tangled, filthy tail. "You're taller," she said.

Star raised his head. "I am?" he replied, surprised.

Bumblewind stood next to him and confirmed it. "Yep, you grew, or else we shrank." Echofrost nickered, amused.

"Maybe you'll grow into those big wings," said Morningleaf. "Come on, we'll walk the rest of the way. Wait until you see Sky Meadow!"

"And the grandmother tree," added Echofrost. "It's huge, and old."

"Is there a lake?" asked Star. "I could use a bath." His friends whinnied in agreement. They trotted the final length of the migration and emerged onto Sky Meadow, the largest grazing field in their territory. Star halted, stunned. He'd never seen such a wide expanse of lush, green grass, and now that he was weaned, it looked delicious. "Incredible," he said, wanting to roll on it.

Morningleaf whinnied. "Isn't it fantastic?"

Star nodded, understanding now why Rockwing was interested in taking Sun Herd's territory.

After the walkers had settled, Thunderwing peppered Grasswing with questions about the migration and the fire, and about Mossberry. The old palomino shook his head, clearly in no mood to answer, but he patiently gave Thunderwing his report until the over-stallion was satisfied.

Morningleaf led Star to a comfortable thicket to rest. As soon as his aching hooves touched the soft, shaded grass, his legs buckled, and he collapsed with a grunt. Echofrost and Bumblewind returned to their mother, but Morningleaf stayed beside Star, grooming the burrs out of his mane as he slept.

When he woke up a few hours later, he was starving. He and Morningleaf grazed in silence until it was almost dark.

"The next migration will be easier," she said. "You'll fly then, I'm sure. The shape of your wings is correct; you just have to grow into them."

"The next migration is after my birthday," Star reminded her.

"So?"

Star shook his head. Morningleaf did not want to believe her sire would execute him, even though the over-stallion had promised it. "Never mind."

Morningleaf ruffled her feathers and changed the subject. "There's a lake down that pathway. Let's go; I think a bath will make you feel as good as new." Morningleaf nodded toward a beaten trail leading out of the meadow.

Star shook his head. "It's too late to swim," he said,

looking at the bright moon over their heads.

Morningleaf curled her lip. "But you smell like mud."

Star nickered, still subdued from his long walk. Sweet-root trotted over to them with her wings full of green shoots. "Eat these," she said to Star. "It's licorice root for your sore muscles." She dropped the roots.

"Thank you," Star said. He chewed the roots, the sharp flavor making him grimace.

"Mossberry was my good friend," Sweetroot said, flicking her chestnut tail, her dark eyes threatening tears. "Grasswing told me you faced the fire and tried to help her. That was brave of you, Star. Thank you." She nuzzled him and trotted back from where she'd come.

"You did that?" asked Morningleaf, looking incredulous.

Star nodded. "But I couldn't save her." He shook off a fly. "Twistfire says I'm bad luck, or worse. What if it's true? What if I am the destroyer?"

Morningleaf nickered. "Nothing that happened is your fault. Not the fire, and not what happened to Mossberry."

"That's what Grasswing said."

"You should listen to him; he's wise. Grasswing, Silvercloud, Dawnfir, and others, they've been talking about you, Star, trying to piece together the legends of previous black foals."

"But all the other black foals—they all died, except for Nightwing."

"As far as we know. But Grasswing thinks the starfire is neutral—that you will get to choose what it transforms you into: a healer or a destroyer. My mother believes the same."

Star ground a root between his teeth, thinking. "But why would Nightwing choose to destroy the herds of Anok? He was loved and protected by his guardian herd. It doesn't make any sense."

Morningleaf sighed. "We may never know why. It was four hundred years ago, but I believe in you. I believe you're going to unite the five herds."

Star's heart raced at her words. The starfire he would inherit felt unreal to him, like a bad dream, but in truth it grew closer every single day. The two friends lay side by side, thinking their separate thoughts, as the moon rose above them.

After a while Star spoke. "Before she died, Mossberry told me the elders believe Nightwing is still alive."

Morningleaf gasped. "What? How?"

"The ancient legends speak of black foals as being—" Star struggled to find the right word. "Immortal."

Morningleaf blinked at him, stunned into silence.

Star continued. "Black foals hibernate when they are tired or injured, but they don't die; at least this is what Mossberry believes." He shook his head. "I mean, believed."

Tears formed in Morningleaf's eyes, making them extra bright. She inhaled sharply, filtering the scents of the night through her nostrils. "That's incredible."

"Then why are you sad?" he asked. "Because of Nightwing?"

"No." Morningleaf looked away. "Because I will die someday, and then you'll be alone."

Star pricked his ears. He'd never thought about the possibility of outliving his friends. He curled his neck over hers. "It's too much to think about right now. Let's just focus on getting me past my first birthday."

He was trying to make her feel better, but her wings sagged, and she looked even more forlorn. Finally she spoke. "So where is Nightwing then, if he's still alive?"

Star stared west, toward the ocean. "The elders think he traveled across the sea to the territory of the Landwalkers, that he's hibernating there." Mossberry had told him that this idea had been passed down to her through the descendants of Spiderwing, one of the few pegasi to survive Nightwing's massacre. Spiderwing was the founding stallion of all the modern pegasi.

Morningleaf swiveled her ears, thinking her thoughts as Star thought his. The Landwalkers on the other side of the ocean were the legendary creatures that tamed beasts, commanded the land to grow their food, and walked upright. No modern pegasus had ever seen one, and it was believed the Landwalkers were unaware of Anok, but stories about the two-legged beings entertained the foals on cold winter nights.

"So Nightwing could wake up?" asked Morningleaf.

Star yawned, exhausted. "I guess so." The Hundred Year Star burned bright in the dark sky, brighter than the moon, and as Star looked up, he caught sight of movement in the rocky foothills. It was Silvercloud with the captain, Oakfire. The pair trotted down into Sky Meadow and separated. A few minutes later they were followed by Grasswing, Dawnfir, and a few others. "What are they doing up there?" he asked.

Morningleaf followed his eyes. "My mother and Grasswing, and the rest, they meet up there at Poppyfeather's Mirror to talk about you, about how to protect you. Thunderwing doesn't know, of course."

Star was surprised. "I had no idea."

Morningleaf nuzzled him. "You're not alone, Star."

He looked away from her, embarrassed and pleased,

and watched his supporters merge back into the herd, careful not to draw attention.

The next day Morningleaf, Star, Echofrost, and Bumblewind left the herd and traveled to Big Sky Lake to swim. Thunderwing's sky patrols kept an eye on them, and all of Sun Herd, from the air.

"Did you hear the news?" said Bumblewind to the group. "Twistfire spotted Mountain Herd steeds on this side of the Blue Mountains. They were spying on us." Bumblewind was breathing hard, partly from excitement and partly from the effort of walking. Star noticed that the pinto colt had grown portly since the weaning in the southern territory.

"I heard," said Morningleaf, pinning her ears. "Those hairy goats better stay off our land."

Echofrost looked nervously toward the Blue Mountains, the northwestern end of Mountain Herd's territory.

Star felt guilty knowing that all this spying and interest from Mountain Herd was because of him. It was unfortunate that the two herds' territories shared such a long border. The thin Vein between them was the only buffer, and to cross it could be considered an act of war by either herd.

The four friends reached Blue Sky Lake and suddenly

forgot all about Mountain Herd. "Look at it!" breathed Echofrost. Star halted. In front of him was the clearest and bluest lake he'd ever seen.

"Last one in is a land horse," whinnied Bumblewind.

Star flattened his ears and galloped toward the lake, determined to be the first one in. He reached the shore and dived under the surface. The water, which fed into the lake from the mountains, was ice-cold.

Morningleaf splashed in above him and then propelled herself down, gliding gracefully next to him. Star kicked, swimming lower, where the light was dim. Two lake salmon flashed by, a blur of pink, and he watched them disappear into the distance. Morningleaf ran out of air and rose to the surface. Star cruised over the sandy bottom, pretending he could fly.

When he surfaced, he sprayed water out of his nose and looked around. Silvercloud had told them that Big Sky Lake was the deepest lake in their territory. The beaches were covered in soft, round pebbles, perfect for rolling on and for scratching backs. Red spruce trees circled the lake, and the dark-blue water reflected the trees and clouds.

Star paddled toward Bumblewind, who was floating and soaking up the sun, eyes closed. Echofrost was flying low over the water, letting her hooves drag and make ripples on the surface.

Suddenly a familiar voice interrupted the peaceful silence. "Look, Stripestorm, it's a flock of ducks." Star looked up and saw Brackentail and his gang buzzing over their heads.

Morningleaf paddled toward shore. "I thought I told you to leave me alone," she whinnied.

Star pricked his ears, wondering when Morningleaf had spoken to Brackentail. It must have been while Star was migrating.

Brackentail and his friends landed. Stripestorm spoke to the fillies, Morningleaf and Echofrost. "Believe it or not, we weren't following you. We came here to swim."

"Let's go," said Brackentail. "They'll be minus one friend soon enough." He shot Star a menacing glance.

Morningleaf tensed, and Brackentail darted out of her striking range.

Star opened his mouth, but Morningleaf whinnied over him, "Someday you'll be sorry you treated him this way, Brackentail."

Brackentail paused, his expression thoughtful. "If the Hundred Year Star turns him into a destroyer, then maybe I will."

Star charged into the brown colt, knocking him down

and straddling him. "I've had enough of you, Brackentail."

The big brown colt rolled to his hooves and flew up in the sky, forcing Star to look up at him. "You want to fight me, Dudwing?"

Star looked at his friends, who shook their heads, begging him not to agree, and then back at Brackentail. "Sure, why not?"

"Star! No!" neighed Morningleaf.

Brackentail hesitated, assessing Star. The big colt hovered, flapping his wings with practiced dexterity, and then he brightened. "You're on. Tomorrow at noon, on the upper flats, we'll finish this."

"Agreed," said Star. Brackentail flew off to swim in the lake, followed by Stripestorm and Flamesky.

Morningleaf faced Star, ears pinned. "What are you thinking, Star? What will you gain by fighting Brackentail?"

Star looked into her glowing eyes, unsure how to explain. "Things with him are only going to get worse if I don't deal with him now."

"Star's right," said Bumblewind, bobbing his head. "It's a stallion thing."

Morningleaf and Echofrost rolled their eyes. "It's ridiculous," said Morningleaf. "And you don't fight a pegasus on the terms he sets, Star. He's going to send you to the golden meadow."

Star swatted a fly with his tail. "It has to be on his terms, Morningleaf. Otherwise it won't mean anything."

She grunted. "It means you're a fool, Star. You're going to lose." She stared at him, unflinching.

"Stay away from me then." Star turned his back on her and trotted home toward Sky Meadow.

His friends followed, and Morningleaf buzzed over his head. "I'm sorry," she said.

He glared at her. "Let's talk tomorrow, after I prove you wrong."

Morningleaf left them and flew home. Bumblewind and Echofrost walked with Star, but none of them spoke. When they arrived at Sky Meadow, Star led them to the cool grass beneath the branches of a weeping willow. Morningleaf landed on the far side of the field and nestled into a deer thicket by herself.

Star already regretted his words and wished Morningleaf would join them, but she was still upset; he could tell by her taut wings. He'd waited over a moon to see her, and now they were separated again because of Brackentail and his useless friends. Star felt precious time passing as each sunrise brought him closer to his dreaded birthday.

7

CANYON RUN

STAR WOKE ABRUPTLY TO THE EYES OF BRACKENTAIL staring in his face. "Good morning," said the brown colt.

Star lurched to his hooves. "What do you want?"

"It's going to be hot later." Brackentail blinked at the sun just cracking the horizon. "I thought we'd get this over with early." He flared his wings in a weak imitation of Thunderwing. Behind Brackentail were his friends, Stripestorm and Flamesky.

Star nodded. "Fine, I'll get Bumblewind."

Brackentail blocked him. "No! There's no time. We're going to the canyons. We have to leave now, between patrols, otherwise they'll see us."

"The canyons? Why not the upper flats like you said?"

"Change of plan," said Brackentail. "I'm challenging you to a hoof race, not a fight."

Star pricked his ears. A hoof race was a contest that favored him. Surely Brackentail knew how fast Star could run—so why would he choose it? Star glanced at the brown colt and noticed he had longer legs than Brackentail's, which meant his kicks had a longer reach. He guessed this was why Brackentail changed his mind, but Star preferred the switch, so he didn't press the colt. "You're on," he said.

Brackentail turned, and Star followed. They trotted out of Sky Meadow into the woods, heading east. Star swiveled his ears, listening for bears or wolves.

They reached the neutral Vein between the territories, and Star halted. The canyons were on the other side of the Vein in Mountain Herd's territory. "What about Rockwing's patrols?" he said.

The brown colt fluttered his orange feathers. "It's fine. They don't watch the canyons; there's no food there."

Star scanned the rising terrain that then flattened into a series of flat mesas and deep crevasses. The few trees and shrubs that marked this wide expanse of rock were dry and tasteless. Brackentail spoke the truth: there was no good food here, and the sky was empty.

"Thunderwing doesn't watch the canyons either,"

Brackentail continued. "We can do what we want."

The colt's dark eyes glittered in the rising sun, and Morningleaf's words echoed in Star's mind: *You don't fight a pegasus on the terms he sets. Well, we're not fighting, we're racing,* Star thought, and he shook Morningleaf's voice out of his head.

"Come on," said Brackentail.

The little group followed him across the Vein and onto the gray rocks. They were slippery under Star's hooves. *This isn't the best terrain for racing,* Star thought. They walked into the canyons, swatting at flies and munching on the few green shoots they could find, climbing higher and higher. When the rocky terrain flattened, Brackentail halted. "This is good," he said. He nodded toward a far tree, the tallest in the area. "The first one to that tree wins," he said.

Star nodded. "If I win, will you leave me and my friends alone?"

Brackentail exhaled. "I'll never bother you again."

Star thought Brackentail's friends looked mildly frightened, but of what—of Star winning? That couldn't be it. He surveyed the canyons, the upper cliffs, and the brightening sky. There was no sign of Rockwing's patrols.

"Flamesky will start us off," said Brackentail.

The red roan filly lifted her emerald wing. Star sidled next to Brackentail, noticing that the brown colt was relaxed, not tensed for running. Star's gut flipped. Something was definitely wrong. Maybe Brackentail was going to cheat by using his wings to propel him forward. Before Star could back out, Brackentail glared at him. "This is for Morningleaf," he said, and then Flamesky dropped her wing and Brackentail surged forward.

Star bolted after him, neck flat, ears pinned, and wings trailing behind him. *For Morningleaf?* What did that mean? His hooves skittered on the slippery rock, but so did Brackentail's. They galloped away to the stifled cheers of the brown colt's friends. Star kept one eye on the sky for Mountain Herd steeds and one on Brackentail. The rock sloped at a gentle angle upward, and Star's long neck pumped with the stride of his legs.

He passed Brackentail, and the thrill of his impending victory fluttered in his belly like a thousand butterflies. He focused on the tall tree and pushed himself faster. Brackentail fell farther behind as Star's hard hooves ate up the distance to the tree.

Suddenly, Star heard shouting, and a smattering of aqua and brown-tipped gold feathers rained from the sky. He looked up and saw Morningleaf and Bumblewind, and his heart soared. They would see him win. It was Morningleaf who was shouting, cheering probably.

Star's hooves struck the ground in one steady beat as he rushed toward the finish line. Brackentail's hoofbeats were far behind him. There was no doubt Star would win.

"Stop!" screamed Morningleaf; her whinny overwhelmed his thundering hooves and his rushing pulse. He lifted his head, and she neighed, "It's a trap." A gust of wind caught Morningleaf's wing and shifted her balance, causing her to roll across the sky. She slammed into a tree and fluttered to the ground, but lifted her head to watch him.

Star dug in his hooves, skidding across the slick rock. He wasn't sure why Morningleaf wanted him to stop, but he didn't doubt she had a good reason. He squinted, and then he noticed the wide divide on the other side of the tree—a deep canyon—and he was sliding toward it. The crevasse was too wide to jump.

Brackentail burst past him and leaped, using his wings to fly him across.

The race was a trick! Star dragged a wing, spun himself around, and skidded backward toward the canyon's edge. Desperate, he sank his teeth into the branches of a large bush just as his back legs slid over the cliff, knocking a flurry of rocks into the open air. His body jerked to a halt before the rest of him dropped over the edge.

Morningleaf, injured from crashing into the tree, limped to his side, and Bumblewind landed next to him. They grabbed his wings in their teeth and heaved Star to safety. The three of them collapsed in a pile at the canyon's edge. Star was wet with sweat and panting. He couldn't speak. None of them could.

Brackentail buzzed over them with his friends, who were trembling. "You lose," said the brown colt, angry. And Star realized that if he'd won the race, he'd be dead, smashed at the bottom of the deep divide—exactly as Brackentail had hoped. The two colts stared each other down, and Star understood he'd been a fool.

"We shouldn't be here," Morningleaf said, glancing toward the sky and ignoring the brown colt. "We need to take cover." She limped toward a grove of trees. Star, Bumblewind, and Brackentail's friends followed her as she struggled and lay down, groaning.

Star noticed that Morningleaf's lower front leg was swollen. "You're hurt," he said through gritted teeth. This was Brackentail's fault.

"We're sorry," said Flamesky to Morningleaf. "We thought it was a joke, that Brackentail would warn Star before he reached the edge of the cliff. We didn't mean to hurt anyone."

"Where's Echofrost?" Morningleaf asked Bumblewind, changing the subject, for which Star was grateful.

"We split up after we crossed into the canyons," said Bumblewind. "I haven't seen her since." They all looked up, scanning the sky for Echofrost. Brackentail refused to join them under the tree. He hovered over their heads.

"We have to find her," said Morningleaf, "and get out of Mountain Herd's territory. What were you thinking, Brackentail?"

The colt flew in a low circle, watching them. "I didn't know you three were going to follow me."

Morningleaf pinned her ears. "You shouldn't be here at all." She staggered to her hooves. "Let's go, but let's stay together."

"Can you fly?" Bumblewind asked Morningleaf.

"I can, but he can't," she said, indicating Star. "And I won't leave him. We'll walk and look for Echofrost. If you want to fly, just stay close."

As they were about to exit the grove, a dappled gray stallion dived from the clouds and smashed into Brackentail, knocking him to the ground. Star's heart plummeted with the colt—the strange stallion was a Mountain Herd steed! Star and the others flailed backward into the trees. Star turned his body, shoving his friends out of view and shielding them as best he could. Suddenly seven more stallions landed beside Brackentail. Star and the others froze, holding their breath.

The steeds were short and muscular and mostly gray in color. They nosed Brackentail to his hooves. "Come with us," said a dark stallion, leaving Brackentail no choice. Star exchanged a terrified glance with Morningleaf, his nostrils flaring as he attempted to steady his breathing. Mountain Herd pegasi were fierce. It was said they lined their caves with the feathers of their enemies.

Star peeked out from his hiding spot and watched the group lift off with Brackentail in tow. They joined a larger group of Mountain Herd pegasi on a ridge far away.

Morningleaf counted the steeds in a whisper. "Silvercloud will want to know everything about them," she said. "There are eighteen under-stallions, four mares, Brackentail, and"—she paused—"who's that?"

Star squinted, following her eyes. Another weanling was standing on the ridge. She was unsteady and silver in color, but tall for a Mountain Herd filly.

Morningleaf gasped. "It's Echofrost! Mountain Herd has captured her too. That's why she didn't make it here."

Bumblewind bleated softly, staring at his captive sister. "Oh no! This is trouble."

"No," said Star, "this is war. We've crossed the Vein, trespassed, and now two weanlings are kidnapped. Someone is going to pay for this."

"Not us," said Bumblewind. "We were just trying to find you."

Star shuddered. "Thunderwing doesn't care about me, but he'll want the weanlings back. And it *is* our fault, Bumblewind. We're in Mountain Herd's territory. Rockwing has the right to take us, and to punish Sun Herd."

"We're doomed," whispered Flamesky.

Morningleaf flattened her ears. "All of you, quiet. This talk is doing us no good. We have to get to Thunderwing. Now."

8

TRAPPED

"MORNINGLEAF IS RIGHT," SAID STAR. HE WATCHED the steeds on the ridge. They appeared to be arguing, stamping their hooves and flapping their wings, but the wind carried off their words. Even from the ground, he could see that Echofrost was trembling, and Brackentail looked like he was shouting at his captors.

"He's going to get himself killed," Star whispered.

As if Brackentail heard Star, he turned his head toward the hiding weanlings and pointed his wing at them.

"Or get *us* killed," said Bumblewind, his voice rising in pitch.

Star's friends swiveled their ears, their eyes rolling,

muscles twitching. He sensed a stampede. "Don't panic."

Suddenly Echofrost squealed from her position on the ridge, and twelve Mountain Herd stallions dived off the cliff, wings wide and shaping the current as they glided toward Star and his friends in the bushes. "They've spotted us!" whinnied Star.

Morningleaf vibrated her wings. "Brackentail ratted us out."

Immediately Flamesky took flight, followed by the rest, retreating toward the Vein and Sun Herd's territory on the other side. Star galloped after them on the ground. Morningleaf flew low, staying near him.

Star shouted at her over the whistling wind. "Go on ahead, and I'll meet you back at the meadow."

"I won't leave you."

Anger sharpened his voice. "Please, do what I say. You're going to get yourself captured if you don't."

The Mountain Herd stallions swooped over him, and Morningleaf swerved out of their way. The biggest gray stallion landed in front of Star, his eyes narrow, his teeth bared. Star slid across the rocks and dodged him by galloping down a steep and narrow canyon trail, his heart pounding faster than his fleeing hooves. The stallion took flight and cut off Morningleaf's path. She veered left and rocketed across the top of the canyon.

"Stop, trespassers," ordered the gray stallion.

Star ignored him and continued down the hard trail into the canyon. It was deep and too narrow for the stallions to fly through, but they followed him from above. Star reached the bottom and galloped, his neck flat and his ears pinned. His lungs were pumping air so fast, they felt ready to burst, and the sounds of his heaving breaths ricocheted off the canyon walls.

As he approached the end of the canyon, Star saw that the Mountain Herd stallions had landed there and were waiting for him. He slowed to a trot, counting six of them. He turned around and saw the other six waiting at the other end. He was trapped. He halted, breathing hard and feeling utterly alone.

"I didn't mean to trespass," he called out, hoping his voice would reach the stallions. "If you let me pass, I'll return home."

He heard amused snorting. "Home?" neighed one stallion. "You're the black foal. No herd wants you."

Star's wings sagged. He knew deep down that this stallion spoke the truth. "Then let me go."

The gray stallion tossed his mane and snorted. "We're Rockwing's border patrol. We have orders to bring trespassers in, black foal or not."

Star sighed. Unless he was ready to make a deal, he doubted Rockwing wanted to see him, but these patrol stallions didn't know that. He hoped Morningleaf had kept flying and escaped. "I won't come out," he said.

He heard a collision above him. He looked up to the top of the canyon wall and saw two stallions yank Morningleaf out of the tree where she'd tried to hide. They dragged her to the very edge of the canyon rim by her wings, and she let out a sharp-pitched, angry squeal. Fury at the stallions and fear for Morningleaf rose in Star's gut.

"There's your friend," said the gray patrol warrior. "We'll bring you both to Rockwing."

Morningleaf blasted one of the stallions in the chest with her hind hoof, but this caused only more amused nickers.

Star knew Thunderwing wouldn't rescue him, but he also knew Rockwing wouldn't hurt him, not as long as he thought he could make a pact with Star. He could save Morningleaf by going with these stallions and convincing them not to take her. "Okay, I'll come out of this canyon if you promise to let her go."

"Star, no. Don't do it," whinnied Morningleaf, struggling with her captors.

Star trotted through the canyon toward the patrol stallions. Time seemed to slow, and he noticed everything. A small mouse, disturbed by his hooves, scurried from under a bush and disappeared down its hole. Far away, the hunting cry of a hawk echoed across the rocks. Beads of sweat trickled slowly down his forehead as the sun's hot rays reached inside the canyon. He wished he and Morningleaf could disappear like the mouse.

Morningleaf watched him, favoring the leg she hurt when she crashed into the tree, holding it at a slant. Her wings were twisted in the stallions' mouths, her pretty blue feathers crushed and wet with saliva. Star realized with sparkling clarity that Brackentail was right. Morningleaf wasn't safe around him. He pinned his ears at the Mountain Herd stallions and stopped several winglengths away from them. "Let her go first."

Without answering him, a silver pegasus dashed forward, just squeezing himself between the narrow canyon walls. Star whirled and bolted, but the stallion grabbed him by the tail. "You promised to let her go," Star said, gnashing his teeth.

The stallions chuckled, and Morningleaf shook her head, her expression disappointed.

"No!" Star whinnied. He tossed his mane as they

dragged him farther out of the canyon, bucking and squealing. He stopped suddenly as a crimson feather floated from above and landed near his hoof. His heart raced when he recognized the unmistakable color: Thunderwing!

Then the over-stallion's trumpeting battle cry pierced Star's ears, causing him to cringe. Star looked up as fifteen Sun Herd warriors swooped over the canyon and descended on the foreign stallions. The silver steed released Star's tail, and Morningleaf was also let go. The tiny filly swooped into the canyon and landed next to Star.

"Look at them," she said, her eyes brimming with relief. Her sire, Thunderwing, and his warriors attacked the Mountain Herd stallions with sharpened hooves and lashing tails. "You see, Star, Sun Herd will protect you."

"I think they're here for you," Star said, skeptical, but also relieved.

Star and Morningleaf crept to the end of the crevasse to watch the sky battle.

"Bumblewind and the others must have made it back and told Thunderwing what happened," Morningleaf said.

From the safety of the rocks, Star saw the Mountain Herd stallions charge, eyes narrowed and muscles bulging. A big gray stallion slammed into Jetfire, causing an explosion of turquoise feathers. Jetfire reared, angling his wings, and bit into the gray's shoulder. The stallion bellowed and bit back, snatching a mouthful of mane. Jetfire struck the gray with a mighty kick, and the patrol warrior careened, head over tail, crashing onto the sharp rocks below with a muted thud.

Thunderwing fought two stallions at once: a gray and a blue roan. They surrounded him, but he dived under them and came up behind the gray. A double kick to his flank sent the stallion rolling across the sky. The blue roan tucked his wings and crashed into Thunderwing. They fell toward the ground, snapping at each other. Thunderwing opened his wings and stepped on the roan stallion, driving him toward land. Right before impact, Thunderwing flew upward, and the stallion smashed onto the ground, breaking his neck immediately.

Thunderwing glided to Oakfire, who was struggling with a dappled stallion and was covered in his own blood. The dapple had kicked him into a daze, and Oakfire was too disoriented to defend himself. Thunderwing rammed the enemy stallion, bit the top of his neck, and threw him into a tree. The branches snapped, and the stallion fell until he regained his wings. He flew out of the tree and hovered, looking around.

Two Mountain Herd stallions were dead, and the rest

were outnumbered.

The dappled stallion called off his warriors and faced Thunderwing. "Leave our territory," he said, breathing hard, his thick hair curled with sweat.

"Not without all my weanlings," said Thunderwing. "The two hiding over there, and the two you took hostage."

The dappled steed snorted. "They trespassed."

Thunderwing hesitated. "Then tell Rockwing I request a meeting."

The Mountain Herd stallion flared his wings. "A meeting?" He circled the dead bodies of his friends. "How about a war?"

Thunderwing grimaced. "Just tell him." He trumpeted for Star and Morningleaf. "Let's go." Thunderwing loped into the woods on hoof so Star could keep up. Jetfire waited for Star and Morningleaf to pass safely by the enemy stallions and then he took up the rear. The group broke into a gallop, with the injured Morningleaf flying just inches off the ground, and they returned to Sun Herd's territory.

9

DIVIDED

THUNDERWING, STAR, AND THE OTHERS GALLOPED
into Sky Meadow like they were on fire. Silvercloud
approached, her wings flared, as the rest of the herd
pranced nervously—their eyes wide with fear. "What happened?" she asked, staring at the blood on the warriors.

"Mountain Herd stallions," Thunderwing said, his
sides heaving.

Sun Herd jolted as if electrified, and four thousand
sets of wings buzzed with rage. Echofrost's dam, Crystalfeather, pinned her ears and opened her wings to lift off,
ready for battle. "Where?"

Star saw her face was etched with grief; she'd been told
her filly was captured. Brackentail's dam, Rowanwood,

looked equally miserable.

"We scared them off, for now," said Jetfire.

He and Thunderwing trotted away to consult with the other captains.

Star and Morningleaf found Bumblewind. He was still out of breath and wheezing. The weight he'd gained since the weaning over a moon ago made it difficult for him to fly, and his belly often cramped with exertion.

Silvercloud pranced to relieve her stress. "Why were you weanlings in the canyons?" she asked.

Thunderwing returned, landing next to them. "No time for that," he said, interrupting. "We have two pegasi in enemy territory." He forced Silvercloud to look at him. "If we can reach them before they reach Rockwing, we might be able to save them, if it's not already too late."

Rowanwood and Crystalfeather sagged against each other and bleated like foals. Star's innards flipped with his thoughts. Rockwing had kidnapped Sun Herd foals before. He'd heard the stories from the elders. Rockwing kept the fillies and killed the colts. One time he'd celebrated his victory by dropping the bodies of the dead foals where Sun Herd grazed, and one of those colts had belonged to Grasswing. Star saw Rowanwood staring at the sky, her eyes bulging. At any moment, Brackentail's body could tumble from the clouds.

Thunderwing summoned his captains, and in minutes they assembled their platoons. Each captain commanded four hundred and fifty under-stallions.

Silvercloud intercepted Thunderwing and pointed at his army. "If you attack them, you'll bring war on Sun Herd." As lead mare, Star knew she had a say in all battles.

Thunderwing listened and then said, "I'm not attacking. I'm rescuing. We killed two of their stallions for these trespassers." He glowered at Star, his daughter, and the other foals. "War is coming whether we attempt to rescue them or not."

Silvercloud turned on Morningleaf, eyes blazing. "Why did you go into their territory? You *know* better. What were you thinking?"

"I—" Morningleaf fought her tears.

"It was my fault," Star interrupted. "I went into the territory, and Morningleaf came to find me."

Thunderwing struck Star with his chest, knocking him across the grass. "You are nothing but trouble, black foal." He swiveled his head to Silvercloud. "You should have let him starve when you had the chance." He pawed the field, churning up the grass. The surrounding Sun Herd steeds lashed their tails.

"Stop!" Grasswing galloped in between Thunderwing and Silvercloud, halting their argument. He turned and addressed Morningleaf. "How many Mountain Herd steeds did you see?"

Morningleaf spoke, her lip quivering. "Twenty-two."

"Mares or stallions?"

"Eighteen stallions and four mares, but now two stallions are dead."

Silvercloud nodded and turned to Thunderwing. "They'll escort the weanlings to Rockwing. We have time. We could send a messenger, try to resolve this peacefully."

Thunderwing opened and closed his crimson wings impatiently. "No. The foals were trespassing, Silvercloud. What is the point of sending a messenger unless we're willing to trade for them?"

"Maybe we *could* trade. They're outgrowing their territory. We could offer them Feather Lake and the pine tree forest in the south."

Sun Herd snorted in outrage.

"For two weanlings?" said Thunderwing. "Never."

"Stop all this talking," neighed Crystalfeather, galloping into the sky. "We're losing time."

Thunderwing ordered her to land. "Calm these mares down," he said to Silvercloud, and then he dismissed all of them and sent his platoons east toward Mountain Herd. He remained to set up a sky patrol over Sky Meadow.

Star and Morningleaf trotted closer to Silvercloud, who stood with wings open as though she were about to fly, or had just landed.

"Are you harmed?" Silvercloud asked.

"My leg," Morningleaf said, looking at it helplessly.

Silvercloud wrapped her wing around her filly's leg. "It's hot and swollen, but I don't think it's broken."

"It's why we stopped to hide. I needed rest," Morningleaf said, looking miserable.

"It's not her fault," said Star. "I shouldn't have followed Brackentail away from the herd. You were right, Morningleaf. I shouldn't have fought him on his terms."

Morningleaf nickered. "Maybe next time you'll listen to me?"

"Maybe," he said halfheartedly.

Sweetroot trotted to them and inspected Morningleaf's leg, causing her to wince. "You need to soak it in cold water," she said. The medicine mare applied chewed-up arnica and offered Morningleaf white willow for the pain. "Don't walk for seven days," she said. "You can stand as much as you like, but no walking; only flying."

The medicine mare flew off to calm the stressed

weanlings and their dams with a mixture of passionflower and chamomile leaves.

"I'll take you to Horsetail Falls," said Silvercloud to her filly.

"I let down my herd, Mama."

Silvercloud exhaled. "You should have told me when you noticed Star was missing this morning, not tried to find him yourself. But you did well to count and sort your attackers under pressure."

Morningleaf was a natural leader—fearless and committed—like Silvercloud, but Star knew Silvercloud didn't want that life for Morningleaf. Being lead mare was thankless and dangerous. Star watched them fly away to Horsetail Falls, where the water was deep and cool.

When they were out of sight, he cantered into the foothills to quench his thirst at Big Sky Lake. Bumblewind followed. After they drank they stood in silence for a while, until finally Star spoke. "Thank you for coming after me in the canyons."

Bumblewind lay in the sand, still looking stunned, but he answered quickly. "You're our friend, Star."

"But look what's happened!" He nodded toward the canyons. "Echofrost and Brackentail are captured."

Bumblewind sighed. "Think what would have happened

if we hadn't come," he said. "If Morningleaf hadn't stopped you, you'd have galloped over the edge of that canyon. You'd be dead."

Star sighed. "That's true, but I'm sorry about Echofrost."

Bumblewind's eyes sparkled with tears. "Thunderwing will get her back."

"I hope so," said Star. He curled up next to Bumblewind in the sand, exhausted. "I can't believe Brackentail tried to kill me," he said, more to himself than to his friend.

Bumblewind folded his wings neatly across his back. "He doesn't believe you're good for the herds, or for Morningleaf."

"Why does he care so much about her? They aren't even friends."

Bumblewind yawned. "I don't know."

Star remembered Brackentail's words right before the race: *This is for Morningleaf,* he'd said. Star shuddered. Brackentail hadn't cared about beating him; the race was an assassination attempt. But why would he think killing Star would help Morningleaf—except for the obvious reason that he seemed to bring the filly bad luck? Nothing the orange-feathered colt did made sense.

Star pricked his ears, noticing the silence. "Bumblewind?"

Next to him, his friend's breathing was deep and calm. Bumblewind had fallen asleep. Star laid his head in the warm sand, just for a moment, and then he also fell asleep.

When Star woke, it was dusk. He nudged Bumblewind, and together they returned to Sky Meadow at a slow walk. Dozens of warriors still patrolled the skies, keeping an eye out for Rockwing. Star entered the meadow to sneering faces.

"It's your fault my son was captured," accused Rowan-wood.

"I told you he's the destroyer," said Twistfire.

Angry pegasi surrounded Star and lashed him with their tails. Star walked through them, tears welling in his eyes as he took the blows, and white flowers sprang up where his tears landed.

"Enough!" bellowed Grasswing and Silvercloud at the same time.

Grasswing galloped to Star's side. "We don't beat our weanlings! No matter who they are."

Twistfire spread his olive-green wings and threw out his chest. "Star doesn't belong to Sun Herd. He has no dam or sire here, and look at the fallen, injured, and captured pegasi in his wake: Lightfeather, Mossberry, Morningleaf, and now Echofrost and Brackentail." Twistfire looked at each steed, his eyes glittering in the twilight. "Who's next?"

A collective shiver ran through the feathers of the Sun Herd pegasi.

"If we kill him right now, the bad luck for the herd will end."

The angry and terrified herd advanced on Star. He crouched, waiting, his heart racing.

Silvercloud shouted over Twistfire. "Which of you will take the blood of the black foal on your hooves?"

Star watched as the fuming steeds exchanged looks and then dropped their buzzing wings. None of them wanted to do the deed themselves.

"It's Thunderwing's place to dispatch of the foal," Silvercloud said, forcing words that brought tears to her eyes. "Which of you will rob our over-stallion of his duty?"

The ferocity of Sun Herd's anger dispersed to quiet grumbling.

Star looked up and saw Thunderwing standing on a mound, letting Silvercloud speak for him. The over-stallion scanned the herd with interest, and no one spoke against her words. "Rest now," Thunderwing commanded his herd, sending them to graze and settle for the night. He trotted to Silvercloud and Star. "You wanted him," he said, nodding toward Star. "Keep a better eye on him."

Star watched Silvercloud and Thunderwing. The stallion's white blaze seemed to glow in the setting sun, and Silvercloud's silver feathers glistened. Star knew she loved Thunderwing, and Thunderwing loved her, but they rarely spoke anymore, and when they did it was to fight.

Star felt sad. The two leaders of Sun Herd had opposing purposes, and this created an impossible divide between them since neither steed would budge.

Star glared at the Hundred Year Star, glowing so impassively and patiently above him. The trouble he caused his guardian herd was happening more and more often, and he knew they were losing tolerance for him. He saw the threats in their eyes, and he believed more attempts on his life would come as the days passed. For the peace of the herd, Star made a decision.

He would have to run away.

10

ESCAPE

A FEW HOURS AFTER SUNSET, STAR HEARD JETFIRE returning with his platoon. The cream-colored captain landed in the center of the herd so abruptly that he startled several pegasi into the sky. His look was grim.

"Give your news," said Thunderwing.

"We spotted the weanlings crossing the Blue Mountains," he said, "but the flight path was too narrow to attempt a rescue. We thought we'd have a better chance after we crossed the pass."

Jetfire stared straight ahead as he spoke, avoiding eye contact with the kidnapped weanlings' mothers. Star saw that his eyes were sparkling, either with tears or fury; it was hard to tell from where he stood.

"When the pass opened up again, it was too late. All of Mountain Herd was grazing below us in a valley of grass. We ducked behind an outcropping of rocks and stayed as long as we could."

Thunderwing twitched with suppressed anger. "What did they do with Brackentail and Echofrost?"

"They were taken straight to Rockwing. He put the weanlings under guard and met with his captains."

Jetfire's words fell on Sun Herd like a heavy blanket of snow. The pegasi shivered in the absolute deadening silence that followed.

Thunderwing nodded. "They are hostages. I expect Rockwing will offer a trade for something of ours."

Under normal circumstances, Rockwing would offer to trade the weanlings for a wingful of Sun Herd fillies, a medicine mare, the detached head of a Sun Herd captain, or rights to a watering hole. But these were not normal circumstances, and Star knew what Rockwing would ask for: himself. Rockwing would try to force Star to make a pact with him in exchange for the lives of the Sun Herd weanlings.

Star took a step forward, and Silvercloud caught his eye. Star guessed she had come to the same conclusion, because she was the one who'd first told him about the ancient belief that a pact could be made with the black foal. It was why Star wasn't too surprised when Rockwing tried to make a deal with him in the first place. If Rockwing partnered with a destroyer, he could rule Anok side by side with him. It was an evil pact, but then, Rockwing *was* evil. And this was one reason why Silvercloud would never allow Sun Herd to trade him for the weanlings.

Star watched as the lead mare nickered quietly to her adult colt, Hazelwind, and Grasswing. They moved silently away from Sun Herd, and Star followed them, curious. They stopped miles later, when they reached Horsetail Falls, where the rushing sound of water covered their voices.

Star stayed hidden but within earshot as they all gathered by the shore. "I believe Rockwing will ask to trade the weanlings for Star," Silvercloud began.

Hazelwind blinked in confusion. "But no herd wants the black foal. Why would he ask for Star?" He stretched his jade wings and refolded them on his back.

Grasswing interjected. "For power, Hazelwind."

"You mean the pact? But that's pure speculation," said Hazelwind.

Silvercloud held up her wing. "Even if Rockwing doesn't ask for Star, the black foal isn't safe here any longer. Thunderwing's patience is worn to the breaking point, and the herd is ready to stampede." She sighed. "I have a plan to save Star, but it's treason, and you know what the punishment is for that."

Star nickered and stepped closer, but still stayed out of sight.

Hazelwind drew in a deep breath and let it out. "Execution."

"Right," said Silvercloud. "You are either in or you're out. If you're out, you should leave now." She looked at each one.

Neither stallion hesitated. "I'm in," said Grasswing.

"Me too," said Hazelwind.

Silvercloud let out her breath. The mist from the falls wet her forelock, and the water dripped down her nose. "Good. I'm going to hide Star. We're leaving tonight."

Tonight? thought Star, and his heart thumped with apprehension.

"Tonight!" said Hazelwind.

Silvercloud tossed her silver mane. "Star isn't safe, and no over-stallion can be trusted with him. He has to be removed from the herds until his birthday."

"Where will you hide him?" asked Hazelwind.

"It's better if you don't know, but I'll need your

help so we can escape."

As the stallions listened to her plan, Star left, heading to the Drink, the big lake north of Sky Meadow. He had to think, to clear his head. He wanted to run away, but not tonight. He wanted one last day with his friends.

Star stood in the shallow end of the lake, letting the cool water soothe his torn feathers. Clouds had blown in, bringing rain, and they masked the light from the moon. He cried silently, his tears dropping into the water where the white flowers could not grow, where there would be no evidence of his terrible sadness.

Suddenly he heard hoofbeats approaching. He tensed, ready to bolt, not sure why he was so afraid. Maybe it was because it was dark and he was alone. Through the developing fog, he glimpsed a mare trotting toward him. He recognized Silvercloud and relaxed.

She coughed to get his attention. He realized she couldn't see him well in the dark, so he lowered his forehead, showing her his big white star.

"What are you doing?" she asked when she caught up to him.

He stared at her for long minutes as the falling rain stuck his forelock to his head. Finally he spoke. "I followed you to Horsetail Falls and heard you talking."

She exhaled. "Then you know I've come to take you away."

"Yes. But do we have to go tonight?"

Silvercloud nuzzled him, her eyes soft. "I'm afraid so, Star. You aren't safe here anymore."

Star and Silvercloud looked up, tilting their ears toward the sky. Hundreds of pegasi flew over their heads and through the rainclouds like bats, scouting the clouds and the horizon for Rockwing's army. If they noticed Silvercloud and Star at all, they would think the two were drinking water at the lake. Star swished his tail. "I just wanted to be alone, but I agree with you, and I was planning to run away, just not tonight."

"I'm sorry, Star, but you can't wait another day. Where were you going to go?"

"Northeast, to the Trap."

Silvercloud gasped. "Pegasi don't live in the Trap; it's too dangerous."

The Trap was a dense forest in the Ice Lands of Anok where the trees were so thick they created an impenetrable ceiling. It was one of the few places in Anok where a pegasus could not be seen from the sky, but it was also so cold even Snow Herd pegasi only traveled there in the summer. And the ceiling of branches and leaves made flying impossible. A pegasus would be forced to escape predators and fires by hoof. But since Star couldn't fly anyway, he knew it would be the perfect place to hide.

"I know, but there is no other choice," Star said.

"Yes, there's a better place," Silvercloud answered.

"Where?"

Silvercloud glanced around the open grass. Pegasi hear very well, and Star guessed she was afraid to say it out loud. "I'll just take you there."

"What about Morningleaf?"

"Hazelwind will watch her until I get back. This is only until you receive your power, Star. Then you can return home."

"I can?"

Silvercloud nickered, shrugging her wings. "I imagine that after you receive the starfire, you'll be able to do whatever you want."

Star shuddered. He hoped he would be a black foal who used the power wisely.

Silvercloud glanced around them. "Now is as good a time as any. Come on; we'll swim out of Sun Herd's territory."

Silvercloud led Star into the Drink. Choppy waves

lapped the rock-strewn shore where Silvercloud entered the water. Star followed her, and when the bottom disappeared beneath his hooves, he swam. The lake was deep and cold and so big that they couldn't see the other side. Pegasi didn't normally travel by water, and the patrols weren't watching the lake, so leaving this way made sense.

"Will Thunderwing try to rescue the weanlings again?" he asked.

Silvercloud shook her head. "They are in the heart of Mountain Herd's territory now; it's too late. War is not worth the lives of two disobedient foals."

Star swam next to her, his face earnest and sad. "What will Rockwing do to them?"

"I believe he'll keep Echofrost alive." She didn't mention the fate of Brackentail. Star nodded, understanding.

An hour later, Silvercloud and Star emerged on the opposite shore of the Drink. They shook off the water and continued at a fast trot to unfreeze their legs after the long, cold swim. Star wished they could travel by air.

They continued into the northern Vein, just south of Snow Herd's territory, and veered west. On rare occasions when the herd leaders met, it was always in the Vein. It was doubtful they would encounter any pegasi here. Star looked up; the moon had traveled far across the night sky, and he was sleepy. But Silvercloud appeared tireless as she eased into an efficient canter, with Star trailing behind her.

"Does Morningleaf know I'm gone?" he asked.

"I didn't tell her," said Silvercloud. "Grasswing is covering for me, and Hazelwind will be with Morningleaf when she wakes up. The story will be that you ran away."

Star jumped over a fallen tree as he followed her. "Morningleaf won't believe that."

"I know, but her confusion and doubt will keep her safe from suspicion."

Star slowed. "What about you?"

Silvercloud turned and gazed at him. Her eyes were unreadable in the dark, and the night felt surreal, like he was dreaming. The rain had stopped at least. Silvercloud changed the subject. "We need to keep moving."

Their journey ended on the rocky coast of Anok. They trotted through tall sand dunes and then down a steep slope to a beach below. Silvercloud broke into a gallop when they reached the shoreline, leading Star north now, up the coast of Anok. Their thudding hooves splashed the edge where the sand met the waves. Soon she stopped, and Star skidded to a halt behind her.

"Where are we?" Star asked.

"This is it," she said, breathing deep and looking into the dark maw of a cave.

"This is what?" he asked.

"Where you'll live for the next four full moons, until your birthday." She led him to the cave's opening, carved into the side of a towering cliff.

Star stopped at the entrance, filtering the dank, salty air over his nostrils and looking doubtful.

"It's safe, Star; I promise."

He took a few skittish steps into the mouth. "How did you know this was here?"

"I found this cave many seasons ago during a council meeting between the lead mares of the five herds," she said. "The meeting was in the Vein between Sun Herd's territory and Snow Herd's, not far from here. After the meeting I took my time traveling home." Silvercloud preened her dusty feathers as she spoke. "I spent a day here at the ocean, resting and relaxing, and I discovered this cave."

Star stood in the cave feeling small and pathetic, even though he was almost as large as she. *Four moons alone!*

He was not looking forward to it.

Silvercloud nuzzled Star, smelling his sweat-soaked hide. "I have to be back by first light," she said. "Grass-wing will cover for me if I'm late, but I'd rather it not come to that."

Star inspected the cave and the hard floor, his ears drooping and heavy.

"You have the same dished nostrils and wide forehead as your mother," Silvercloud said.

"I wish she were alive."

Silvercloud flexed her wings, preparing to leave. "In all my years, I've never known a mare more proud of her foal than Lightfeather was of you."

Star brightened at her words.

"Don't worry; you'll be safe here, and I'll come back for you after your birthday, okay? Until then you're going to have to take care of yourself."

They pressed their foreheads together, and Star bleated his sadness.

"Patrols of Sun Herd pegasi will be scouting for you as soon as they know you're gone," Silvercloud said. "They'll search everywhere, including the Vein. When the other herds find out you're missing, they'll join the hunt. No one can save you, and no one can help you. But you have to survive. Do you understand?"

Star swallowed, fighting tears. "I do," he said.

Silvercloud nodded, then took off as Star stood, small and alone in the mouth of the cave.

11

PUNISHMENT

MORNINGLEAF WOKE TO THE FLURRY OF WING-beats. She looked toward the commotion, her heart stalling. Rockwing soared over Sky Meadow accompanied by a small battalion of warriors. She skittered to her hooves and whinnied softly for her mother.

"Shh," her brother Hazelwind said.

"Where's Mama? Where's Star?"

"Silvercloud is over there." He nodded toward their mother, who was across the meadow, standing with Grasswing. Silvercloud's face was solemn and her body deathly still. "What has she done?" asked Morningleaf.

"She hid Star," Hazelwind said, his voice as quiet as a summer breeze.

Morningleaf's jaw dropped. "Where? Why?"

Suddenly the herd became restless. Hazelwind and Morningleaf glanced up to see the over-stallion of Mountain Herd and a few of his warriors descending in a slow circle. Hazelwind whispered, "To keep him safe. Listen."

Thunderwing assembled four warrior battalions and surrounded Rockwing when he landed. Rockwing, outnumbered by his enemies, stood with one leg resting, looking unconcerned.

"Rockwing should be afraid," said Morningleaf.

Hazelwind snorted. "I've seen him in battle; nothing scares him."

"You may speak," Thunderwing said to Rockwing.

Rockwing stretched his wings and refolded them. He took his time, eyeing the mares and fillies with interest.

Morningleaf and Hazelwind watched their father's muscles twitch. The Sun Herd warriors curled their lips, showing their teeth, but they held steady, waiting. When Rockwing spoke, his voice was as commanding as Thunderwing's. "Your weanlings trespassed into my territory, and your warriors killed two of my stallions. In return, I want the black foal."

Morningleaf lost her breath. "No." She surged forward.

Hazelwind tackled her, whispering in her ear, "This is

why she hid him; now be quiet."

Morningleaf peeked at her mother. Except for the occasional spasmodic twitch of her wing, Silvercloud stood as still as a stone beside Grasswing. Fear overwhelmed Morningleaf like a swelling river overrunning its banks. She twisted free of Hazelwind and cantered to her mother, drawing the eye of Rockwing.

Thunderwing distracted the foreign stallion. "You can't have the colt," he said.

Rockwing flared his wings. "I'm offering a trade."

Thunderwing shook his mane. "Keep the weanlings."

Crystalfeather and Rowanwood bleated in outrage.

Thunderwing whirled on them, ears pinned, neck coiled like a snake. "They broke the law," he snapped. The mares hunched and slunk away.

The rest of Sun Herd pranced in place, threatening to bolt, or worse, to stampede into the sky. Thunderwing whinnied an order, grounding all of them.

"You won't trade?" said Rockwing, curious.

"I won't." Thunderwing lashed his tail.

"All right then, have it your way." His last words rumbled forth in a low growl, and Morningleaf's feathers stood on end. Rockwing was declaring war—not outright, but it was coming. She leaned into her mother and watched

Rockwing and his warriors gallop into the clouds.

Rage detonated Sun Herd, and Twistfire led the crusade. He knew Thunderwing wouldn't trade the colt, so he and a band of stallions confronted Silvercloud and Morningleaf. "Give us the black foal."

Silvercloud shook her head. "I don't know what you are talking about."

Twistfire reared, threatening Silvercloud. "The weanlings' deaths will be on your wings if you don't give him up. Where is he?"

Thousands of eyes scanned Sky Meadow, everyone searching for Star.

Thunderwing landed in a flurry of red feathers along with Jetfire. "What's going on here?"

Twistfire arched his neck. "I'll trade the black foal myself if you won't."

Thunderwing's expression blackened, and Morningleaf crouched in her sire's shadow. "Sun Herd won't trade the black foal," he said. "We are the guardian herd. It is our responsibility to protect him or destroy him."

"Not to trade him is to abandon the weanlings," said Twistfire with unmasked hostility. "Or has your mate convinced you that the foal is good?"

Thunderwing kicked Twistfire so hard and fast that

Morningleaf didn't see the strike, only the effect of it. Twistfire flew over backward and landed upside down on his wings.

"Put him under guard," said Thunderwing. Jetfire took custody of Twistfire.

Morningleaf stayed close to her mother. The whole world seemed upside down. The adults were fighting, Star was gone, and innocent weanlings were in danger. "Why didn't he trade Star?" Morningleaf asked Silvercloud, confused. "He hates him." Maybe her father was starting to believe.

Silvercloud read her thoughts. "Nothing has changed, Morningleaf. Rockwing wants to make a pact with Star, to rule Anok. He's hoping Star is the destroyer. Your father knows that, and I guess he's decided not to take the chance of it happening, not even for the lives of the weanlings. The rest of Sun Herd doesn't understand. They are ruled by emotion, and they aren't looking into the future. Besides, Star was born to our herd, and it's Thunderwing's duty to . . . handle him—no matter what."

"You mean kill him."

Silvercloud didn't answer.

Morningleaf glared at the Hundred Year Star blazing above their heads. "Are you sure he's safe, Mama?"

"Yes, I think so."

Thunderwing held a brief meeting with his captains and then returned to Silvercloud. "Give me the colt," he said. "I'll keep him safe until his birthday."

The irony of his words was not lost on Morningleaf or her mother. Silvercloud lifted her chin in defiance. "Until he's a yearling, Star is a foal and under my protection."

Their eyes locked, and Morningleaf watched her parents argue without speaking. Over twenty years together had erased the need for words—their relationship was like a deep river: calm at the top but always moving below, carving the land between them. Finally her father spoke. "Where is he?" he asked, his tone grim.

Her mother merely shrugged her silver wings.

Thunderwing turned on Morningleaf. "Tell me where to find him."

She trembled. "I don't know, Father."

Thunderwing paused, looking at them. "So be it," he said, and he flew to his captains, ordered the formation of search parties, and dispatched them to look for Star.

"It's happening," whispered Morningleaf, her belly crawling like she'd eaten a mouthful of bugs. "They're going to find out what you did."

Silvercloud exhaled. "Just stay calm."

Two days passed, and the search parties failed to find Star. Thunderwing interrogated Sun Herd one by one. Finally it was Bumblewind who cracked; he'd seen Silvercloud leave with Star.

Thunderwing exploded and confronted Morningleaf's mother. "Bumblewind says he saw you and Star heading to the Drink the night of the kidnapping. He says you returned and Star didn't."

Bumblewind sulked nearby, and Morningleaf saw guilt and fear in his eyes, but his sister was missing, and Bumblewind thought Star was the key to getting her back. Morningleaf couldn't really blame him for telling.

But Silvercloud said nothing.

Thunderwing lashed his tail. "You didn't lose him, Silvercloud. You hid him; now everyone knows it."

"I hid him where you'll never find him," Silvercloud admitted.

Thunderwing crashed his wings together, sending crimson feathers floating over the grass. "You should have let the foal die with his mother." Bitterness sharpened Morningleaf's father's voice. "It would have been natural, and we would not be dealing with this now. Do you understand the consequences of what you've done?"

Silvercloud nodded, tears welling in her eyes.

"If he's the destroyer, you have condemned us all to death." Thunderwing sagged, defeated. "This is treason, Silvercloud."

Silvercloud nodded again, and Morningleaf braced herself. The punishment for treason was execution.

"No!" Bumblewind cried. "I'm sorry, Silvercloud. I just—I just want Echofrost back."

A whimper escaped Morningleaf's lips, and Silvercloud's attention snapped back to her filly. "You're all Star has left," she said to Morningleaf. "Hold steady."

Morningleaf choked back her tears and nodded.

Thunderwing turned to Silvercloud. A lead mare had never committed treason before in anyone's memory. While it was punishable by death, the killing of a mate was forbidden. Morningleaf wondered what her father would do. She shuddered, remembering a nightmare she'd had—one in which her sire choked her, his own filly, and then snapped her neck.

"Silvercloud, daughter of Seaheart, you are banished from Sun Herd for the rest of your life. You are no longer Silvercloud, lead mare of Sun Herd. You are now

Silverlake, lone mare of no herd." Thunderwing spoke without a trace of emotion.

The Sun Herd steeds flapped their wings, whispering. Banishment was a fate worse than death.

"Father!" cried Morningleaf, charging him. "No, please."

Thunderwing blocked her with his wings. "Someday you'll understand," he said.

Morningleaf faced him, her chin firm, jaw clenched. "I hope I never do!" She turned around and flew toward her mother.

Silvercloud, now Silverlake, sagged, and Morningleaf darted to her side, relieved her mother wouldn't be killed but terrified too. Pegasi didn't survive long alone, and of course contact with Sun Herd would be forbidden.

"You will leave in the morning," said Thunderwing. "Whoever loves you has one night to say good-bye." With that he flew away.

It was a long night for Morningleaf and Silverlake. Hundreds of pegasi came to pay their respects and to say good-bye. Sweetroot reviewed all the possible medicines Silverlake might need in the wild, including one to take her life if she grew weary of the loneliness.

Silverlake shook her head. "I won't need that."

When the procession was over, Silverlake snuggled with her filly. Morningleaf fell asleep, and when she woke, her mother was gone.

Morningleaf rested under the willow tree all day, thinking and crying. This was where Star had sought shade after their first fight. For such a helpless foal, he'd made quite a mark on Sun Herd. They were broken and fighting and on the brink of war with Mountain Herd. If Star were the healer, how could such destruction follow in his wake?

12

CRABWING

IT WAS LATE MORNING ON THE COAST OF ANOK, and it had been a moon since Silvercloud had left Star at the cave. Star trudged through the deep sand, heading to the river to drink. He panted from the exertion and the weight of his wings. Halfway to the river he had to lie down to rest. Star's bones ached, and his stomach had stopped grumbling days ago. He was past the point of hunger. He was starving.

He spent his days searching the dunes and cliff paths for vegetation. He dug up roots with his hooves, ate the bottom leaves off the stout coastal trees, and munched on dune grasses, swallowing sand by the mouthful. The sand was making him sick. Sharp pain stabbed his gut, and the only remedy for it was to walk some more. This added to his exhaustion and his need for more food. It was a vicious cycle, and one he couldn't continue much longer.

He hadn't seen a single pegasus, and that was good. He slept in his cave at night and again during the hottest part of the day, when the sand burned the tender centers of his hooves. He'd also struck up a friendship with a seabird. He'd inadvertently stepped on a shell one morning, cracking it with his hoof, and the gull swooped down from the sky to eat the meat; then he cocked his gray head at Star, seeming to say, "Can you do that again?" And so Star did, and it became a game between them. Star cracked shells, and the gull ate the meat. The bird was unafraid of Star and inquisitive. Sometimes he slept at the mouth of the cave, and Star named him Crabwing.

On his way to the river, Star looked up at the sky. The low sun was hot and blinding, compounding his misery. Finally he reached the river's mouth, which fed directly into an ocean bay. He drank more than he needed, letting the water fill his empty stomach. There was no greenery left by the river; he'd picked it clean. He sighed; he'd have to travel up the cliffs to the dunes to look for something to eat.

He raised his wings as much as he could and wished

yet again he could fly. Silvercloud might have enjoyed her time at the beach because she wasn't stuck on the ground. If he remembered right, the nearest grazing was a day's journey away by hoof, but she could have flown there and back in an hour. He'd considered abandoning his sea cave and moving inland where food was plentiful, but he knew patrols of pegasi warriors were searching for him, and Silvercloud had ordered him to stay by the cave.

Star panted by the river and rested; just looking at the steep path leading up to the dunes made him weary. He turned his head. Birds squawked and dived into the water, popping back up with small fish and plants in their beaks. The ocean was placid today.

He closed his eyes, deciding to nap before he searched for food. He stretched out and believed he would be content if he never moved again. His body was ready to quit, and his mind was close behind. He snorted at his predicament: he was starving to death and bony, he couldn't fly, he was sick, and his best friend was a bird. He wasn't much of a pegasus, let alone the mightiest of them all. Even Crabwing could fly; although the more Star fed him, the less the bird chose to do so.

If he died here beside this river, the herds of Anok would continue as they had for another hundred years.

He assumed he was the healer, but there was always the chance he was the other, and he wouldn't know for sure until his birthday. He'd been told what to expect. At midnight the Hundred Year Star would flare in the sky, transfer all its light to him, and then disappear for another hundred years. He would receive his inheritance and become the most powerful pegasus in Anok.

Since Nightwing had never showed any signs of aggression until he received his power, it was assumed that the black foal had no choice about what he would become. Star shuddered at the thought that he would turn violent like Nightwing and kill innocent pegasi. He fully understood Sun Herd's fears, because thousands of pegasi had once believed wrongly in Nightwing.

Star let the gentle swish of the nearby waves lull him into a trance. Perhaps he would look for food later, perhaps he wouldn't. He sprawled out on the riverbank and relaxed. He was exposed to every kind of danger here, but his ears gave up their constant swivel, and he closed his eyes, shutting off the panoramic view of his surroundings. He let the flies crawl onto his hide, as it took too much effort to swish them off with his tail. Before long he was asleep.

When Star woke, it was afternoon, and his hide felt

like it was on fire. Startled out of his melancholy, he jolted to his hooves. He was covered in sand fleas, and they were biting him. He shook himself hard. The bugs were too small to be dislodged. They scurried through his hide, and he realized they were eating him alive. In a panic, Star galloped into the icy bay and paddled to deep water. Hundreds of sand bugs floated off him, and the rest congregated on his back. The intensity of the biting increased, as though the bugs realized they didn't have much time left with Star. He arched his back in pain and dived under the surface.

He opened his eyes in the clear water. He could see the outline of the entire bay and the dark blue of the open ocean beyond. The bay floor was carpeted with smooth stones, and fish were either scarce or his sudden plunge had scared them away. Star stayed under as long as he could to rid himself of the bugs, and then he surfaced and found himself in a massive floating bed of kelp.

He hadn't been paying attention, and the kelp bed must have drifted over him. Now long pieces of seaweed were draped over his ears and wings, threatening to entangle him. He used his teeth to remove a large piece off his back, and as he bit into the fibrous plant, the flavor of it awakened his tongue, and he realized it was food.

He chewed the kelp, swallowed, and waited. Long minutes passed before he decided that it agreed with him, and then he gorged himself.

The nutrition of it coursed through him like rain after a drought, and his body cried out for more. The kelp bed was massive, and on the other side of the bay he saw another one. Star whinnied with pleasure. He ate until his tummy ached, and then, careful not to move too fast, he swam back to shore and rested on the bank, content and free of bugs. He had no doubt now that he could survive here until his birthday.

Star returned to the bay every day for swimming and meals. He discovered delicious sea grasses and even tastier red kelp to round out his diet. He found a tall oyster reef for Crabwing. He peeled the creatures off the reef with his teeth and cracked them on a large, flat rock with his hoof, causing the insides to ooze from the shell. Crabwing followed Star and sat in the sand each day to wait for his meals. The bird grew fat and lazy, and was soon riding on Star's back to travel to and from the cave. He amused Star, who couldn't believe the bird would choose to ride when he could fly.

It wasn't long before Star began to feel strong again. His body rounded, his coat became glossy with good health, and the sharp pains in his stomach disappeared. The salt water did wonders for his feathers, thoroughly cleaning them and removing the dandruff. Within a half a moon, the underwater-flying sessions had strengthened his shoulders enough that he could tuck his wings on his back. He was also growing into his long legs. One day, while admiring his shadowy profile, he said to Crabwing, "Look at me; I look like a flying pegasus."

"Squawk," said Crabwing, dancing in the sand.

Suddenly, and without warning, cold rain dumped from the sky, and Star was soaked in seconds. Star nickered to his bird. "That's what I get for admiring myself. Come on, Crabwing, let's go." Star extended his wing, and the small, gray gull walked up his feathers and settled onto Star's back. Star loped to his cave, seeking shelter.

As the days continued to pass, each one seeming the same as the last, Star focused on making his cave as comfortable as possible. He collected dried seaweed for his bed, and he made a nest for Crabwing. The seaweed served to soften the floor and provide him with midnight snacks, and he stored oysters in the coolest section of the cave so Crabwing could also have late-night snacks.

Fall was over, and it was winter now, so it rained—a cold, biting rain—almost every day. On one such day, Star and Crabwing nestled at the mouth of the cave together and watched the rain pound the sand. Star munched on dried kelp and cracked oysters for Crabwing. He offered the bird some of his greenery, but the gull wasn't interested. Crabwing pushed an oyster shell under Star's nose with his beak and squawked. Star obliged him, shucking out the meat with his teeth. "What are you going to do when I'm gone?" he asked.

Crabwing considered him with his small, glittering eyes.

"You're going to have to hunt on your own again."

Crabwing squawked and pushed another shell at Star, who tossed his mane and snorted. "You are a demanding little bird, Crabwing." Star fed him and returned to watching the rain. He wondered what was happening back home in Sky Meadow. He hoped Silvercloud had returned undiscovered. He could imagine Thunderwing's fury when he realized Star was gone.

He closed his eyes and thought of his friends. Morningleaf would be worried about him. Poor Echofrost was kidnapped, and it was all because of Brackentail. Star wondered why pegasi were so afraid of him when they were destroyers themselves. Thunderwing, Brackentail, Twistfire, and Rockwing—it seemed they lived for death.

Crabwing stood and fluffed his feathers. He jumped onto Star's back and nestled between his warm black wings to sleep. It hadn't taken the bird long to realize that Star's body made a nicer nest than dried seaweed.

Far in the distance, Star spotted a tall fin that cut through the ocean waves, followed by four more: killer whales. A pod of them enjoyed hunting off the coast, and he saw them often. The waves were big today. Between the rain and the deafening roar of the surf, he couldn't hear anything else. Star enjoyed swimming in the bay, but the open ocean frightened him. It could be fierce or gentle, welcoming or dangerous, peaceful or voracious, but whatever it chose to be, it wasn't something he could control and so he stayed away from it.

Once Star received his power, the herds of Anok wouldn't be able to control him, and he realized that was the source of their fear. The pegasi weren't afraid of destruction after all; they were afraid of powerlessness. Star contemplated this for a long time. Crabwing nestled deeper between his wings, and Star turned his head to look at the small white-and-gray bird. He could crush Crabwing under his hoof as easily as he cracked the oyster shells, and yet he had gained the creature's complete trust.

Star gazed over the sea, which was dark and unforgiving. He stayed away from the ocean because it didn't care about him. It was something to respect, not to befriend. Crabwing trusted him because Star chose not to wield his greater strength over the bird. If he could gain the trust of Crabwing, maybe he could eventually gain the trust of the pegasi of Anok.

13

SNOW HERD

"I WONDER WHERE STAR IS AND WHAT HE'S doing?" Morningleaf said to Bumblewind and Grasswing. It was late afternoon in Anok. Thousands of sparrows chattered in the oak trees, and insects buzzed from flower to flower in Sky Meadow. Morningleaf, Bumblewind, and Grasswing were grazing quietly together.

"I think he's in the Vein," said Bumblewind.

"Let's not speak of where we think he is or what he might be doing," Grasswing said, lashing his tail at Bumblewind. "The meadow has ears."

Morningleaf wished her father were more like Grasswing. The palomino stallion was stern but kind.

"What do you think Echofrost is doing right now?"

asked Bumblewind.

"No doubt she's more miserable and more frightened than we are," Morningleaf said.

Across Sky Meadow, Thunderwing prepared the stallions for war, even the yearlings. He drilled them from sunrise to sunset. If the over-stallions of the other herds found out he'd lost track of the black foal, he could be executed, and Thunderwing wasn't going to let that happen without a fight.

A shadow of wings crossed over the field, and a Sun Herd stallion let out a sharp peal of alarm. Morningleaf tucked her tail and galloped to the weeping willow tree for cover. She peeked through the branches and saw an envoy of pegasi from Snow Herd. Bumblewind charged into her, breathing hard, and halted. The two friends watched the strange pegasi approach.

Their massive shoulders powered wide-set wings that carried their thick bodies through the air. Their hides were white, light gray, or cream colored, with pale feathers. Morningleaf didn't think they were raiders; there were too few of them for that.

Besides, the envoy consisted of mares, stallions, and even a weanling. The presence of the young colt was their proof they meant no harm. They circled Sky Meadow until

Thunderwing signaled his permission for them to land.

"That's Icewing," whispered Dawnfir. She and the others had joined the weanlings under the tree. Grasswing nodded in affirmation.

Morningleaf studied the over-stallion of Snow Herd. Since Icewing was Lightfeather's sire, that meant he was Star's grandsire. He was a stunning dark-silver pegasus with a white mane and a shimmering tail. It fell in loose ringlets like Star's tail. His feathers were powder blue and so were his eyes. He was thick and hairy, but his muzzle was refined for a steed his size. The large white star on his forehead was in the same shape as Star's.

As was customary for dignitaries from other herds, the envoy was given rest and led to water before Thunderwing demanded the reason for their visit. Standing next to Icewing, Morningleaf saw her father in a new light. Maybe he was so tough because his enemies were so tough. Both stallions were designed for battle, with heavy muscles, rock-hard hooves, and powerful jaws. Thunderwing was taller than the Snow Herd over-stallion but leaner.

Her father's warriors could dispatch of the envoy in a few bloody minutes, but Icewing had taken quite a risk to come here himself, and her father would hear him out. Once the Snow Herd pegasi had replenished themselves with grass and water, Thunderwing invited them to approach him.

Icewing had not requested a private meeting, so most of Sun Herd jostled for a position to listen. It was rare for Morningleaf to wield her status as the over-stallion's daughter, but today she did. Pegasi made way for her as she flew to a spot at the front of the herd. Bumblewind followed and landed at her side. Grasswing pushed his way through the herd and stood with them. They had a perfect view of the over-stallions.

Thunderwing and Icewing faced each other, and neither flinched nor even seemed to breathe. After moments of silence Thunderwing finally said, "You have traveled a long distance, Icewing; tell us why you have come. Do you seek our assistance?"

Morningleaf glanced at the silver over-stallion for his reaction.

Icewing snorted. "Snow Herd requires no assistance. I've come to claim my heir and daughter, Lightfeather. My mate drove her off when she was a filly, and I've heard she lives here."

A collective murmur and flutter of wings rippled through Sun Herd. Morningleaf whispered to Bumblewind, "I thought this was going to be about Star."

Thunderwing rattled his feathers. "Why do you come for her now, after such a long time without her?"

Icewing lifted his head, but his wings slumped, looking heavy and sad. "I've no foals left, no heirs. She's of age to join with a stallion and continue our line." Icewing narrowed his eyes. "If I leave here without her, I will return and take her by force."

Morningleaf sucked in her breath. "Icewing doesn't know Lightfeather is dead," she whispered to Bumblewind.

Thunderwing flared his crimson wings. "It's been too long. Lightfeather is a Sun Herd mare now. You have no claim on her, heir or not."

Icewing twitched, and Morningleaf believed it took all the stallion's willpower not to clobber her father over the head.

"What does he mean, 'heir'?" asked Bumblewind.

Grasswing answered. "Snow Herd and Desert Herd track their lineages. Lightfeather and Frostfire are the last foals in Icewing's line, and both were driven from Snow Herd by his mate, Petalcloud."

"No, there is another," said Morningleaf, eyes wide. "Star is Icewing's grandson."

Grasswing pricked his ears. "You're right, but if Thunderwing won't let Icewing claim Lightfeather, he won't let him claim her colt either—not that Icewing would want Star."

Bumblewind eyed the impressive silver stallion. "It's hard to believe he only had two foals."

Morningleaf knew the stories. Icewing's mate was Rockwing's traitorous daughter, Petalcloud. She was ambitious and wanted to be a lead mare, but this couldn't happen in Mountain Herd, where her father was over-stallion. To gain her freedom from Mountain Herd, Petalcloud promised to give Rockwing her firstborn colt. Rockwing had two fillies, but all his colts had been born dead. He accepted Petalcloud's deal and let her leave.

Petalcloud then traveled to Snow Herd, where Ice-wing was the new over-stallion and had not yet chosen a lead mare. She convinced him to choose her without tell-ing him about her deal with her sire. The cunning mare kept her promise to Rockwing and gave her firstborn colt, Frostfire, to him. Icewing was furious, but unable to stop it without declaring war. After that Petalcloud and Ice-wing had six more foals, and like her sire's foals, all six were born dead.

In frustration, Icewing sired Lightfeather with another mare. When Petalcloud found out, she drove Lightfeather and her dam out of Snow Herd. Lightfeather's mother was killed by a bear, and several days later a Sun Herd patrol found the little white filly hiding in a tree, and they rescued her. That was many, many seasons ago, and long before Morningleaf's birth, but the stories about Lightfeather were Morningleaf's favorites.

Thunderwing snorted, bringing Morningleaf out of her thoughts, and he abruptly ended the argument with Icewing over the adopted filly. "She is not your heir any longer. Lightfeather is dead."

This news took Icewing off guard, and he reared back. "Dead? Why didn't you send a messenger?"

Thunderwing stamped his front hooves. His captains tensed, and Icewing's entourage splayed their wings. Morningleaf tensed too. If this meeting got out of control, she would have a front-row view of a massacre. She held her ground and memorized the conversation. If she ever saw Silverlake again, her mother would want to know every detail.

Thunderwing tempered his fury. "Why would I send a messenger to Snow Herd? My mate adopted Lightfeather. She became our filly."

Icewing matched the words with rearing and stamping of hooves. His dense coat was wet with sweat in the heat. "I'm her sire."

"I raised her."

Morningleaf pricked her ears, noticing that her father's eyes were sad. She and Star were born the same night, and neither of them had known Lightfeather for more than a few hours, but Thunderwing had known the white mare almost her whole life. Morningleaf wondered for the first time how Thunderwing felt when Star's birth killed his adopted daughter. He was angry, everyone knew that, but maybe he was also terribly sad.

Icewing flared his wings, his battle muscles twitching. It was clear to Morningleaf that this was not going to end well, but the same realization must have dawned on Icewing, along with the knowledge that he didn't have enough steeds with him to do battle. Icewing softened. "It's common courtesy to send a death message, even for a stolen or adopted foal."

Thunderwing lowered his wings, also seeming to decide against battle. "That's true," he said, and the tension between the stallions eased. Morningleaf was glad. With Rockwing threatening them over the hills, it wasn't a good time to pick a fight with another herd.

Icewing folded his wings, mollified. "Please tell me how she died."

The Sun Herd steeds shifted, tensing. Lightfeather's

death was not something they liked to remember, but Thunderwing did not mince words. "She died birthing the black foal."

Icewing staggered backward as though Thunderwing had kicked him in the gut. "My daughter is the mother of the black foal?"

"Was," corrected Thunderwing. "And there is your solace. If you had claimed the filly while she was still alive, the black foal would be your problem right now and not mine."

Icewing's jaw gaped, and he was unable to speak. One of his under-stallions requested a water break. Morningleaf noticed that all the thick-coated steeds were dripping with sweat. Thunderwing agreed. The Snow Herd envoy met in the shade of the grandmother oak tree to speak in private.

Morningleaf watched Icewing lean on another stallion, his eyes round and rimmed in white. She'd never seen an over-stallion overcome by any emotion other than anger.

Sun Herd went back to grazing until Icewing was ready to meet with Thunderwing again. The silver stallion's attitude had changed. "I thank you for raising my daughter, Thunderwing, and I relinquish my claim on her."

"I'm sure you'll see her soon enough in the golden meadow," Thunderwing said, mocking Icewing's old age.

Grasswing lashed his tail, speaking to Morningleaf and Bumblewind. "That coward!"

"Who?" asked Morningleaf.

"Icewing—he's afraid to claim Lightfeather now, afraid it will mean Snow Herd is the rightful guardian herd of Star."

Morningleaf considered his words and was glad Star wasn't here to witness his own grandsire denying him. "It's not even necessary to cut ties with Lightfeather and Star," she said, grumbling. "Star was born to Sun Herd; that makes him ours."

"True," said Grasswing, "but in a herd that tracks lineage, it matters."

Icewing now seemed embarrassed by his visit, and he ignored Thunderwing's comment about his age. "Before we leave, I'd like to see Lightfeather's colt, the black foal, and take news of him to Snow Herd."

A hush fell over the meadow.

Morningleaf knew Star's life was the business of every pegasus in Anok, so her father could not deny Icewing's request.

"What is it?" asked Icewing. "Did he die too?"

"Not yet," said Thunderwing. "He escaped."

Icewing reeled, and Morningleaf wondered if the old silver stallion could handle another shock. He recovered and thrust his chest toward Thunderwing. "You lost the black foal of Anok?" Icewing peered into the sky, as though Star might be flying there.

Thunderwing arched his neck. "He's not up there. He can't fly."

"You lost a weanling who can't fly," Icewing sputtered. "How is that possible?"

Thunderwing narrowed his eyes and refused to answer.

Icewing folded his wings and shook his head. "Were you going to tell the herds, or does your reluctance to send messages extend to all matters?"

Thunderwing had made the biggest error of his life when he lost track of Star, and Morningleaf watched him eat Icewing's insults. Morningleaf wondered why Thunderwing didn't lie. She could only guess it was because he knew he would be found out sooner or later.

"I will send messengers to the herds," said Thunderwing. "This just happened."

"Can you explain to me how it happened?" Icewing asked this without hostility but with open curiosity.

Thunderwing sighed. "It was my mate, Silverlake. She nursed him after Lightfeather died. He's her milk son, and she hid him to protect him."

Icewing, whose mate had also betrayed him, nodded. "Where is Silverlake now?"

"I banished her for her treason," said Thunderwing, pinning his ears.

Placated, Icewing ruffled his feathers. "I'll send the messengers to the other herds."

"No, I will," insisted Thunderwing.

Icewing arched his neck. "We both will. And I'm going to suggest that each herd form patrols to search for the foal. One of the herds will find him, and then we'll meet back here on his birthday so you can execute him—in case you need our assistance."

Thunderwing's hooves danced in anger, but he absorbed the parting slur.

Icewing commanded his envoy to kick off. The Snow Herd steeds galloped into the sky just as the sun set over the sea in the west.

14

CRABWING'S ROCK

CRABWING SQUAWKED, WAKING STAR OUT OF A dreamless sleep. The black foal lifted his head, yawning, and looked outside in time to see the sun split the horizon. Crabwing always woke Star at dawn.

Almost three full cycles of the moon had passed since the day Star discovered the kelp, and he'd spent those days gorging on seaweed, swimming in the bay, and feeding Crabwing. He was mildly concerned about his pet bird. Star hadn't seen Crabwing fly in days. The little fellow rode on Star's back or waddled on the ground. Star wondered if it was laziness, or if his friend was too fat to fly. He knew he should feed Crabwing less, but Crabwing pestered him incessantly for more food.

Star emerged from the cave and stretched. Crabwing followed, waddling and pecking at empty shells. The ocean shimmered in the early-morning light. Star extended his wing to the bird, and Crabwing walked up his laddered feathers and settled onto Star's back. Star trotted toward the bay, with Crabwing squawking encouragement. When they arrived, Crabwing fluttered to the ground, or maybe he fell—it was hard for Star to tell the difference.

Despite the breeze the bay was placid today, and the water was extra clear. Star stared at his reflection in the water. It seemed that all he had done was grow in the last moon. His proportions were evening out, and he looked like a regular pegasus now. The legs and wings that had been so obnoxiously oversize now fit his larger body. His chest was deep, and his neck had developed the proud arch of a stallion. Pleased as he was, he did wish he were smaller. Stallions didn't like other stallions who were larger than they were, and Star didn't need to add to his long list of undesirable qualities.

But he was most excited about his wings—he could unfurl them and tuck them at will, and he practiced this every day. It was a basic maneuver that foals mastered by their third moon, but it was new for him. For most of his life his wings had dragged on the ground. He'd been taunted and bullied, and he'd endured endless applications of Sweetroot's balms to heal his tattered feathers and ease the constant pain between his shoulder blades. Now his feathers were shiny and intact to the ends of his bones. He couldn't wait for Morningleaf to see him.

Crabwing whistled, breaking Star's reverie.

"I know, you're hungry," Star said to the bird.

Crabwing bobbed his head and hopped from foot to foot, excited.

Star trotted into the bay, swam like a duck for a few minutes adjusting to the icy water, and then dived under. This was his playground. He extended his wings and flapped, propelling himself to great speed. He circled the entire bay once, doing a safety check. Now and then seals or small sharks swam into the brackish water, but today he saw only fish.

Star swam to the oyster reef and snatched half a dozen shells in his teeth. He returned to the shore and dropped them on Crabwing's rock—the large, flat stone he used every day to feed his bird. He lined up the shells while Crabwing danced in the sand.

"Here you are," Star said, cracking each one with practiced finesse and then backing away. The oyster bodies oozed out of the broken shells and dripped over the edge of the rock, slimy and white. Crabwing scooped them up, threw back his head, and guzzled the juicy mess, flapping his wings with delight while he ate.

Star nickered, amused. "When you're finished, I'll get you some more."

Star returned to the water; it was his turn to eat. He paddled to a thick bed of floating red kelp and floated into the middle of it, munching the salty plants contentedly.

Suddenly something beneath the surface bumped Star's hoof, causing his heart to thrum in his chest. He paddled in a circle but couldn't see through the dense layer of kelp. He could tell that it wasn't the nudge of a curious fish. It was something much larger. It bumped him again, spinning him around.

Star quickly paddled toward shore, nostrils flared, but he couldn't smell anything except the sea. His widened eyes scanned the surface as a large wake of ripples appeared. Whatever was under the water was huge. Star tucked his tail, unsure of what to do.

He stopped paddling, but the creature bumped him again, and then three black dorsal fins emerged from the water right in front of him. Star's stomach flipped at the sight. He turned toward shore, and two more fins rose from the depths. He was surrounded.

Star steeled himself and dived under to face the threat. Six killer whales stared back at him, their eyes bright with intelligence. A chill slid from Star's ears to his hooves. He had watched this pod hunt and kill a shark not long after he'd arrived at the cave. They were dangerous, but hopefully not hungry. As if answering that question, the six orcas swam past him as though interested in something else.

Afraid to turn his back, Star watched them. Their heavy, shapeless bodies were graceful and powerful underwater. The killer whales swam to the bottom of the bay where the flooring of smooth stones was thickest and took turns swimming upside down over them. Star understood immediately—they were scratching their backs! He'd figured out this same trick himself, only he performed it on the shore. Rolling on smooth, round pebbles provided a comfortable way to reach between his wings. Star lifted his nose out of the water to breathe but kept his eyes trained on the whales. Slowly he paddled backward toward the shore.

The whales made pass after pass over the rocks, taking turns. Then one broke away from the pod and pumped his tail, gliding toward Star, which sent his heart racing again. The whale circled him, curious, and Star's gut twisted. It was close enough to bite him if it chose. As soon as his hooves touched the sand, he turned and fled onto the beach.

He panted and shook the water out of his eyes, his legs quaking. "Did you see that, Crabwing?"

Star looked up and found himself face-to-face with five strange pegasi stallions standing on the shore. They were adults and warriors, as evidenced by their extensive battle scars. And since all five had feathers in varying shades of green, yellow, and brown, Star knew they had come from Jungle Herd.

Star blinked at them, stunned.

He was taller than four of them, and the warriors took a step back, their eyes wide with surprise. "He's big," whispered one.

Star's heart sank; he'd been found.

"The black foal of Anok," the leader said, appraising Star's frame. He was the eldest of the five. They raked their eyes over Star's body, nostrils dilated, wings flared. Star realized that most pegasi lived their whole lives without ever seeing a black foal.

"He's a weanling?" asked another.

The leader stamped his hoof in rebuke. "He's nothing." He gazed at Star with cold hatred in his eyes. "I'm

Snakewing, over-stallion of Jungle Herd. You will come with us, black foal."

"No. I won't go with you," Star said. "I'm not afraid of you." But Star was afraid, and he didn't know what to do. He was still a weanling, and he couldn't fly.

Snakewing looked straight at Crabwing, who had trotted across the sand when he saw Star. "We've been watching you two all morning," he said.

Star's spine tingled.

"Squawk!" It was as if Crabwing knew they were talking about him. He danced on his flat rock, cocking his head. Star wished his bird would fly away.

Snakewing bared his teeth. "You will come with us now. You have no choice." With a lightning-fast strike, Snakewing clubbed Crabwing with his hoof, spilling the gull's guts across the stone.

"No! Crabwing!" Star thrust his body between the bird and the over-stallion, but he was too late. Snakewing's hoof had crushed the bird. Crabwing was dead, stretched across the rock, his bright eyes now as gray as the sky.

Rage sent fire through Star's muscles. He wheeled around and kicked Snakewing in the chest, sending the stallion flying across the sand. Snakewing recovered and whinnied the call to attack. The five Jungle Herd stallions unfolded their wings and charged.

Star bolted, galloping up the shore to the sand dunes. Images of Crabwing, split open and bleeding, blinded him, but his instincts and familiarity with the land guided him.

He was fast on land, but the warriors caught him easily by air. A brown stallion with pale-yellow feathers kicked Star's flank, causing him to cry out. A second warrior joined in, and they pummeled Star's back and neck with sharp blows. Star spread his wings, shielding his spine, and raced across the dunes.

The warriors took turns dropping on him and striking him, trying to reach his head. Star pinned his ears and ran faster through the dunes, his breath loud in his ears, with no thought as to where he was heading. He dodged most of their kicks, but he couldn't focus, and he couldn't fight back unless they landed and faced him. And even then there were five of them and one of him. He had to get away.

Star raced down the coast alongside the high cliffs. The ocean raged far below on his right, and the foothills rose on his left. He'd exited the dunes and was now galloping on hard ground. He picked up speed, his legs a blur. All the days spent trotting through deep sand and swimming had made him strong and efficient. He felt he could run all day, and it looked like he would have to, because the five warriors were equally tireless in the air.

Without speaking, the five of them suddenly veered and flew high above him. Star switched course and galloped to the foothills, where he hoped he would find cover. The stallions regrouped, and three of them landed in front of him.

Star dropped his haunches and slid to a halt, just avoiding them. He whirled around and ran back the way he'd come, with the warriors chasing him on land. The other two flew beside him. They left only one path open. They took turns biting his rear. Star lashed at them with his thick tail.

With his ears pinned, his neck stretched flat out, and his legs hitting the ground in almost one beat, Star couldn't run a hair faster. He thundered across the plateau, and, too late, he realized they were herding him in the direction they wanted him to run. He racked his brain for a reason why. Perhaps there was an ambush ahead, a gang of Jungle Herd warriors waiting to tear him to shreds.

Fury cleared his mind and wiped away the horror of Crabwing so he could think again. The ground ahead was clear of large trees, rocks, and hills—there was no place for a pegasus, let alone a gang of them, to hide. They were herding him up the side of a small hill; the ambush was probably over the crest of it where he couldn't see. But there was nowhere left to go, so Star decided to keep running. He would meet his fate head-on.

The bites on his rear let up a bit when the stallions realized he was going toward the trap. Star prepared for battle. If nothing else, he wouldn't be the only pegasus to die today. He crested the hill, and what he saw sucked the air out of his lungs. Instead of charging into a mob of angry pegasi, he galloped over the edge of a cliff into thin, cool air.

Star fell, head over tail, weightless and helpless. He saw the warriors leaning over the edge of the cliff nickering in amusement, and then his somersaulting body showed him a view of the beach as it raced to greet him. Star envisioned Brackentail's hateful smirk. *It's just like what happened in the canyon run,* he thought. *I fell for it again.* Star closed his eyes. *So this is how it ends.* Then a vision of a beautiful white mare, Lightfeather, sprang into his mind. She bit his ear hard. "Fly!" she whinnied.

Star's eyes sprang open. He immediately opened his wings, and they caught the air seconds before he hit the beach. His speed caused him to rocket over the waves. He careened from side to side, straining to hold the bend in his wings. He wasn't exactly flying, but he wasn't exactly falling either. He was gliding!

Star whooped, causing a minor shift in his feathers that sent him tilting sideways. He curled his wings over the current and pushed down, righting himself. Behind him, the Jungle Herd steeds glided down from the cliff, following him.

Star flapped harder while trying to keep his path stable. Flying was a lot like swimming. He angled his wings like he did underwater and turned toward shore. His control was shaky, but he soared to the beach, landed with a stumble, and gathered his bearings. The Jungle Herd stallions dropped gracefully next to him.

"Why did you run if you could fly?" asked a dark bay captain with emerald feathers.

Star folded his wings, silent, refusing to answer to his enemies.

Snakewing snorted. "Because he didn't know he could." The over-stallion lashed his tail. "Congratulations, warriors, we just taught the black foal how to fly."

The group shifted uneasily. The balance of power between them had just tilted toward the black foal.

Even Star understood the significance of Snakewing's

words: he was bigger, faster, and maybe stronger than most warriors, and now he could also fly. Star exhaled. It was hard to believe that the enormous wings he'd been dragging around since he was born had, in seconds, become his greatest asset. Now that he could fly, he could probably evade capture until after his birthday. He could be safe—unless Snakewing did something immediately to stop him.

Snakewing must have had the same thought. The over-stallion reared, and Star ducked at the same time. Snakewing's sharpened hoof came down, just missing Star's head but striking a hard blow to Star's shoulder, crippling him with pain. The other four warriors surged forward and rained blows on Star from all directions.

The strike to his shoulder stung so badly that he couldn't lift his wing, so Star used his teeth to attack. Snakewing rammed him. If Star went down, he'd be trampled. He splayed his legs and swung in a circle, surrounded and overwhelmed.

Snakewing landed a clean strike to Star's flank, slicing open the skin. Star collapsed and covered his head. The warriors went in for the kill, but Star rolled, knocking one down, and regained his hooves. He saw Snakewing's vicious expression, and without planning it, Star reared and struck Snakewing with an over-stallion's deathblow. The resounding smack ricocheted off the cliff wall and echoed over the open ocean.

The attack on Star stopped. He uncovered his face and saw Snakewing gasping at the water's edge. He had nailed the stallion right between his eyes and split open his skull. Blood poured from the wound and colored the surf red. "Did I do that?" Star asked out loud.

The Jungle Herd stallions backed away, perplexed. Their over-stallion was bleeding to death, and Star had delivered the deathblow.

When a stallion killed an over-stallion, it meant he could take over that stallion's herd and command his warriors. But Star was just a weanling, too young to become an over-stallion. The Jungle Herd warriors stared at Star, unsure how to proceed with their leader dying and without anyone to take charge.

"Help me," rasped Snakewing.

Star stared at the dying stallion. The excitement and fear of battle drained from him, leaving only the painful throb of his wounds that sent chills through his body. He didn't like seeing his enemy defeated this way.

A rush of sound fractured the silence, and one of the under-stallions screamed. Star saw the movement just in time to stumble out of its path. A killer whale, the largest from this morning, charged the beach. It slid up the shallow waves, mouth open. Star glimpsed its white teeth, gleaming like sharpened pearls, and then it seized Snakewing in its jaws.

"No!" the warriors screamed as Star looked on in horror.

The over-stallion bucked inside its mouth, bleating like a colt. The orca contracted its muscles and used the downward slope of the sand to inch its way to deeper water. When it could, it turned and swam away, with Snakewing clenched firmly in its teeth. The last thing Star saw were his dark eyes, glazed over from terror and the loss of blood, before he vanished under the waves. Bubbles burst the surface, and then a wide ring of blood appeared.

Star sat on his haunches, shaking violently.

The youngest Jungle Herd stallion turned in fear and pointed his wing at Star. "Did you see that?" he said to his friends. "He controls the beasts in the sea. He's the destroyer."

The other three nodded, and all four backed away from Star, not daring to take their eyes off him. Star caught his breath, unable to comprehend the impact of the day's events.

When the four stallions reached a safe distance from Star, they fled up the face of the cliff and disappeared over the edge.

Star sat in the sand until all the blood began to make him feel ill. "What has happened?" he whispered to himself.

He limped home to his cave, lay down on his bed of seaweed, and cried silently in the dark—for Crabwing, for his mother, for the captured weanlings, for Mossberry, and even for Snakewing.

The destruction in his wake was undeniable. Star had to wonder about his true nature. His birthday was only seven days away, and then he would know.

It was time to leave the cave in spite of Silvercloud's orders to stay put. The Jungle Herd pegasi would report his hiding spot when they returned. He wasn't safe here anymore.

15

WAR

MORNINGLEAF GRAZED WITH BUMBLEWIND AND
Grasswing in the center of Sky Meadow. Bumblewind
kicked the trampled grassland. "It's no good; I'm still
hungry."

Morningleaf scanned the herd; the steeds were dull
coated and thin. Because of all the foreign patrols in the
sky, Thunderwing only let them travel in assigned groups
to outer meadows and clearings where the grass was better. Their group left twice a day with Jetfire, but she knew
no steed in Sun Herd was getting enough to eat.

Morningleaf fanned her wings, noticing how the gold
light from the star made her aqua feathers look green.
After Star's birthday, the Hundred Year Star would be

gone, spring would come, and it would be time for Sun Herd to migrate back to their grazing lands in the south; but Morningleaf had a recurring, unsettling feeling that she wouldn't be around to make the journey.

Next to her, Bumblewind grumbled. "I can't believe your father joined with her," he said, casting a baleful look at the new lead mare, Maplecloud.

Grasswing nosed him in the shoulder so hard he almost fell over.

Morningleaf sighed. "It's okay, Grasswing; he can talk about it." Her father had held an emergency joining ceremony after her mother's banishment, and Maplecloud became his new lead mare.

"She's strong and smart," said Grasswing, "a sensible choice for your father."

"And conniving," muttered Morningleaf. But she knew that being lead mare was dangerous, and most mares wanted no part of it. Maplecloud would now be held responsible for the foals and the mares, and for the lost steeds. In a war she'd captain the battle mares. Silverlake had said yes to Thunderwing out of her unshakable sense of responsibility, but Morningleaf suspected Maplecloud did it for power.

"Well, he didn't join with her for her looks," said

Bumblewind, making Morningleaf choke on a mouthful of grass.

Grasswing nodded toward Thunderwing, who was gliding overhead, surveying his herd. "It doesn't matter why he chose her, but it had to be done. Losing the black foal has made your father look weak. An attack is coming. I feel it in my bones." Grasswing ripped a dry plant out of the soil and chewed it thoughtfully.

Morningleaf refolded her wings. She was probably the only steed in Anok who was looking forward to Star's birthday. If he destroyed the over-stallions, her mother's banishment would be lifted. If he united the herds, the same would occur. She didn't care about the rest of it.

"But Maplecloud is cruel," said Bumblewind.

Grasswing sighed. "She gets the job done."

"They're made for each other," said Morningleaf with a sad sigh. Maplecloud was a blond buckskin mare with dirt-colored wings. Her mane and tail were black, and her head was thick and shapeless. She had big teeth, and she used them often to nip disobedient yearlings. Morningleaf didn't like anything about her.

A snowfall of feathers drew Morningleaf's attention skyward. A pegasus mare rocketed overhead, her neck flat, her ears pinned, and her wings tucked. Seven Sun

Herd warriors pursued her, closing in on her.

The frazzled herd stampeded into the sky, and the walkers galloped to Grasswing. Thunderwing rose to meet the approaching mare, and Maplecloud whinnied her first command to Sun Herd. "Land and hold steady," she said. Her voice was shrill and it left Morningleaf with an ache behind her eyeballs, but the herd obeyed.

Morningleaf and her father recognized the frantic mare at the same time. It was Silverlake.

"Mama!" Morningleaf cried, and flew to her mother's side.

Silverlake made an ungraceful landing next to Thunderwing. The Sun Herd warriors dropped next to her and then surrounded her. "She came from the direction of Mountain Herd. She's alone," their captain, Twistfire, said.

Thunderwing bared his teeth. "I thought you went to live with the black foal." His comment served to remind everyone how she'd lost her position as lead mare. Maplecloud joined them, and she stood possessively at Thunderwing's right shoulder. Morningleaf watched understanding flicker across her mother's face when she saw the mare with Thunderwing. Morningleaf glanced at her father and thought he looked embarrassed.

"No. I've been hiding in the Blue Mountains, living

with land horses," replied Silverlake.

Morningleaf nuzzled her mother, drinking in her warm, familiar scent. The faint odor of the horses still clung to her mother's mane and tail.

"You have broken your banishment by returning here, Silverlake." Thunderwing shook his head, angry and disappointed. "You know that the consequence for breaking banishment is death."

"I haven't just been hiding," said Silverlake, panting. "I've been spying on Mountain Herd. You must gather and prepare. Rockwing has assembled an army. He's going to attack Sun Herd."

Thunderwing tensed. "When?"

"Within the hour."

"How many?"

"Three thousand strong, all warrior stallions. They're just over the second ridge in the Blue Mountains."

"Three thousand? Rockwing doesn't have that many warriors in his herd."

Silverlake exhaled; the look in her eyes was grim. "It's not just Rockwing attacking us. He's joined with Snow Herd, Desert Herd, and Jungle Herd."

Thunderwing pinned his ears. "Over a few trespassing weanlings?"

Silverlake shook her head. "I don't know. But there are enough of them to annihilate us."

Grasswing whinnied. "I can guess Icewing is behind this. After informing the herds we lost the black foal, he must have convinced them to unite and attack us."

Thunderwing nodded in agreement. "And when it's over, Rockwing will claim our grazing lands so he can expand the size of his herd."

"He's wanted our lands since he became over-stallion." Grasswing tossed his mane and narrowed his eyes, scanning the faces of all the gathered steeds. "We're not just fighting for Echofrost and Brackentail anymore; we're fighting for all of Sun Herd."

The Sun Herd pegasi paused in stunned silence. A current of ferocity and rage flowed through the herd, lacing the air with static energy, and Morningleaf's heart jolted into a fast gallop. The elders said pegasi were created for war, and from where Morningleaf stood, that seemed to be true.

Orders immediately flew, and the steeds exploded into action. Morningleaf and Bumblewind darted out of their way. Fifteen hundred warriors grouped into their platoons, and fifty new under-captains were deputized; one of them was her brother, Hazelwind. In spite of his self-proclaimed desire for peace, Morningleaf noticed he jumped at the invitation to lead a platoon, and she shook her head. Pegasi claimed to desire peace, but they always seemed to seek war.

The strongest mares, about nine hundred of them, assembled in front of Maplecloud, and she divided them into troops. She appointed captains and marched through their ranks calling out orders.

Morningleaf saw Crystalfeather. The chestnut mare flexed her wings, each muscle tense, and she obeyed the buckskin mare's every command. Maplecloud had made her a captain.

Morningleaf swiveled her ears and took another look at Maplecloud, realizing how well the mare's nasty temper suited her with war just moments away. She was powerful, hard-nosed, confident, and ready to give her life for Sun Herd, and suddenly her father's choice made sense.

Maplecloud dispatched the elders to collect the weanlings and hide them in the forest. Sweetroot and a white yearling stallion named Ripplebreeze shared the command for this group. Sweetroot led Morningleaf, Bumblewind, and the rest into the relative safety of the trees, and Ripplebreeze took up the rear. As they exited the meadow, Silverlake landed next to her filly and laid her head over Morningleaf's neck.

"Mama, I'm scared!" Morningleaf said.

Silverlake took a long whiff of Morningleaf's flaxen mane. "I know, but no matter what you see today, stay hidden. Star can't fulfill his destiny without you. I've been thinking," said Silverlake. "Why does the Hundred Year Star send such a helpless foal to receive such great power? Have you wondered about that?"

"Of course," said Morningleaf, "because it doesn't make any sense. Most black foals die the day they are born."

"That's right. The only way Star can live is with help from the herds. This makes us complicit in his destiny, which is our destiny too. I think his powerlessness is a test of our character, not his, and the herd has been cruel to him, Morningleaf. It will get worse before it gets better, and without you, I'm not sure he'll make it."

"But I can't protect him."

"Not to protect him, Morningleaf, to remind him of who he is, and who he can be. This battle will be the worst thing you've seen in your life, but don't let it fool you. It doesn't matter; the winner doesn't matter. All that matters is that you survive until Star receives his power."

"Why me?"

Her mother pressed her forehead against Morningleaf's.

"Because you believe he's the healer, and the rest of us just hope he is. There's a difference, and he can feel it."

Morningleaf nodded. "I understand."

"Good." The silver mare glanced across Sky Meadow, where Sun Herd was flexed for war. "It will be best for you if you don't watch this."

Morningleaf fought back her tears. It felt like her mother was saying good-bye to her, again. "Yes, Mama."

Silverlake nuzzled her daughter, unable to say another word, and then she flew away to join the battle mares.

Sweetroot settled the weanlings in the dense forest. She nudged Morningleaf into a thicket of brush. Morningleaf had to lie down to fit under the branches. She was invisible from the air, but she couldn't see the meadow or anything else, just Sweetroot's old, cracked hooves.

Then the sentries whinnied in alarm. Rockwing's army was approaching. Morningleaf chewed her lip and considered her options. Her mother had told her to stay put, but she couldn't just hide under a bush until the battle was over, and she had only a few seconds to change locations before the fighting began. She knew a place where she'd be safe and where she could watch the battle.

Knowing she was doing something very stupid and unable to stop herself, Morningleaf flew out of the brush right under Sweetroot's nose. The old mare nickered in surprise, but she was too late. Morningleaf swooped through the trees, dodging branches, flying sideways, and emerged into the Sky Meadow in a blur of aqua wings. She scanned the field as she zipped past. She'd learned from Silverlake how to estimate large numbers of pegasi quickly. Morningleaf estimated there was a total of twenty-four hundred Sun Herd warriors and battle mares in Sky Meadow, and then she disappeared into a hollow halfway up the big grandmother tree. She was just small enough to squeeze inside.

Only Grasswing noticed her. He stared into the hole and straight into her heart, and guilt washed over her. Silverlake had ordered her to stay alive, and she'd reacted by disobeying. But Grasswing didn't look angry. He nodded his head, seeming to say he would watch out for her as best he could. Maybe he thought she was incredibly brave, or maybe incredibly dumb. Her father said they were two words for the same thing sometimes.

The Sun Herd battalion kicked off, darkening the grassy field. The forest creatures tensed, and even the wind seemed to pay attention as the winged steeds created their own powerful currents. Their excited whinnying and snorting grew into a steady rumble that drowned out the chattering of the birds.

Four hundred and fifty battle mares, led by Maplecloud, peeled off and flew west, away from the fight.
Morningleaf watched them disappear, confused. The other
half of their group peeled off and flew east. The warrior
stallions remained and formed a long line in the sky facing the lands of the Mountain Herd.

They flapped their wings furiously, hovering in place
and scanning the horizon, their wings beating as one and
their expressions fierce. Then, sweeping down from the
canyons, Rockwing's army appeared. Even in the distance,
it was clear they were bigger, stronger, and faster. Snow
Herd, Jungle Herd, and Desert Herd had contributed only
their best and largest warriors to the battle.

Morningleaf recognized the herds by color. Snow Herd
was predominantly white, Mountain Herd was gray,
Jungle Herd was brown, and Desert Herd consisted pri-
marily of buckskins and palominos in varying shades
of gold. Her Sun Herd warriors spanned the spectrum
of colors in the five herds, but their vibrant feathers set
them apart, shining and sparkling like bright stones
underwater.

These same wings now buzzed in anticipation with
the first glimpse of Rockwing's army, the great size

disadvantage stoking rather than killing their excitement. Thunderwing flew in front of the line, ordering his stallions to hold. His crimson feathers fell like drops of blood on the grass. Morningleaf's awe flipped to fear and threatened to choke her. She suddenly wished she were back in the thicket.

16

FEATHERS AND BLOOD

SILVERLAKE WATCHED THE BATTLE MARES PEEL away and fly in opposite directions. She decided it would confuse them if she joined their ranks, so she stayed to fight with the stallions.

"Go into the woods," Thunderwing ordered her. But Silverlake was not a Sun Herd steed anymore, and she didn't have to follow his orders. She stayed, hovering behind the front line.

Rockwing's army flew just over the treetops, their ears and necks flat, their freshly sharpened hooves coiled, and their tails lashing. Silverlake narrowed her eyes and bared her teeth.

When Rockwing's front line crossed the boundary of

Sky Meadow, Thunderwing released his warriors. They flew forward with a deafening battle cry, Silverlake surging with them. The two armies clashed in a collision of exploding feathers and piercing screams.

The front lines locked together, and Silverlake waited for the first stallions to break through. She trained her eyes on the enemy as injured warriors from each side thudded to the ground. Sharpened hooves sliced through flesh and bone, and snapping jaws ripped wings to shreds. Blood pooled in the grass, and the smell of it wafted to Silverlake, causing her lips to curl.

The front line finally broke, and the stallions separated, fighting in clumps at varying altitudes. Grasswing and the healthiest of the walkers pranced below. They finished off any enemies who fell to the grass still alive. All around, the warriors were silent except for their grunts and death cries. Bloody feathers drifted across the meadow like ash.

A heavy gray stallion charged Silverlake, his hooves extended. She tilted, flying sideways, dodging him, and then she whipped around and circled over him, landing a kick to his head that drove him toward the field. Grasswing leaped in the air, snatched the stallion's wing, and hurled him toward his walkers, who clubbed the stallion until he was still.

Grasswing looked up, checking on her.

Silverlake's heartbeat thudded in her ears, and she was breathing fast, like she'd just jumped into an icy lake, and every sense was sharpened as she surveyed the field.

To her left, Flamesky's dam, Violetsun, battled a white stallion. Silverlake charged forward to help her. They flew circles around him, biting into his hide and ripping at his feathers. The stallion spun like a foal chasing his tail, but he was unable to catch the smaller mares. His blood splattered Silverlake's feathers.

Violetsun rammed his flank. He flipped head over wing. The two mares sliced into his belly with their hooves. He trumpeted his rage and frustration. Silverlake and Violetsun pelted him with hard kicks, trying to finish him fast before his friends came to help him.

Then Violetsun grabbed the stallion's tail in her teeth. But with a violent whip of it, the stallion hurled her into the grandmother tree. The hard trunk broke her back. Violetsun slid down the bark and landed at its base, dead. The white stallion faced Silverlake, jaws open. He was so close she could feel the heat radiating off him.

"You're next," he said, panting.

And then crimson feathers blocked her vision. She

darted out of the way, and Thunderwing crushed the stallion's skull in one swift blow. Her ex-mate touched noses with her and then flew away to fight with Jetfire.

Silverlake dropped to the ground, gasping for air. She assessed the sky. Rockwing's army was slaughtering Sun Herd, and rage flooded her muscles with new energy. She kicked off and attacked the smallest stallion she could find. He didn't see her coming, and she broke his wing with one swift blow that sent him careening into the forest.

She scanned the sky, looking for her next victim, and whinnied at what she saw. The nine hundred mares who'd left before the battle started must have circled around, because now they were rocketing over the hills and closing in on the rear of Rockwing's army. Maplecloud's battle cry and fresh troops revitalized Sun Herd. Thunderwing joined his new mate, and all Sun Herd rallied against Rockwing.

The mares took down hundreds of stallions before the surprise of their ambush wore off. Even Rockwing appeared stunned. If Silverlake hadn't been banished, she wouldn't have been able to warn Sun Herd about the war, and Rockwing would have found them unaware and grazing. Instead he'd met a herd with a plan.

Silverlake turned just in time to see Brackentail's sire, Ashfire, receive a deathblow to the head and crash onto the grass. Earlier, Stripestorm's mother was killed by a Desert Herd steed, and Flamesky's mother died when her back was broken. Silverlake had been wrong when she told Morningleaf this battle didn't matter—it mattered to all the orphans.

Where was her best friend, Crystalfeather? Silverlake set off to look for the chestnut mare.

On her way she passed Thunderwing. He was in the throes of a battle against three Jungle Herd stallions. They had him surrounded, but Thunderwing wasn't an over-stallion just because he was handsome; he was also the most accomplished fighter in Sun Herd. He dispatched all three of his attackers with ease and flew off looking for more.

Silverlake searched for Crystalfeather. She found her quickly, but she was being attacked by a stallion from Snow Herd. Silverlake pinned her ears and darted across the meadow to help her.

Crystalfeather had sunk her teeth into the silver stallion's wing. "I got the other one," Silverlake neighed, snatching his free wing. Crystalfeather bucked and kicked the stallion in the chest so hard she stopped his heart. He slumped to the grass, eyes open and blank.

"Thanks," Crystalfeather said, panting.

All around Silverlake, battling warriors were landing, too exhausted to fight in the air. All battles eventually ended on the ground, which meant it was almost over. And Sun Herd just didn't have enough warriors to win this one.

Silverlake pricked her ears as a fresh battle cry erupted from Grasswing. His walkers weren't tired yet. They galloped into the fray, their useless wings tucked but their sharp hooves and teeth bared for battle. Grasswing pranced forward, his neck arched, his tail high, and his crippled wings spread wide to make him look larger. He crashed through the meadow delivering deathblows with practiced finesse.

Silverlake and Crystalfeather fought tail-to-tail, spinning in a circle and biting any stallion who came too close. Then a shadow blocked the sun, and dark-blue and gray feathers floated over the grass. Rockwing landed in the meadow.

Without hesitation, Grasswing charged the over-stallion. Silverlake looked for Thunderwing, but he and Jetfire were busy fighting four Snow Herd stallions.

Grasswing and Rockwing circled each other, muscles

twitching. Rockwing's respect for the crippled palomino spoke volumes about Grasswing's skill in battle. If his wings still worked, he could be over-stallion of Sun Herd, but Silverlake knew he'd never wanted that.

The warriors battling near the two stallions paused in a temporary, unspoken truce so they could watch the two legends face off. Everyone knew Rockwing had stolen Grasswing's colt, Graythorn, broken his wings, and dropped him from the clouds.

Now Grasswing challenged his old enemy—not to steal Rockwing's authority, but for revenge. The murder of the colt had linked these two stallions for forty-two seasons, and the heart of it beat between them like a living thing. Their dispute would be settled today.

Grasswing pinned his ears and charged. Rockwing rushed to meet him, and their chests clashed like a clap of thunder. Rockwing snapped at Grasswing, who ducked. The palomino clamped his jaws around Rockwing's knee, causing the stallion to scream.

"That's for Graythorn," he snorted. Pegasi all over the meadow stopped fighting to watch.

Rockwing reared, pulling his leg free, and then kicked Grasswing in the neck. The palomino somersaulted from the force of it, and his head smashed into a rock, dazing him. Grasswing struggled to his hooves. Rockwing took flight to take the pressure off his injured knee. Grasswing looked up at him, bracing.

Rockwing dived at the palomino, battering him with his hooves. Grasswing reared and tried to pull the stallion out of the sky. Silverlake tensed, wanting to help, but Hazelwind held her back. "Look around you," he said. "This is the final battle."

She looked and saw no one was fighting anymore. All wings were tucked. Sometimes it happened in a war that a fight between two could settle a battle between many. Whoever won would win the whole thing, as long as no one interfered.

Silverlake stepped back and folded her wings, more tense than ever.

Grasswing leaped, grabbed a mouthful of Rockwing's tail, and slammed him onto the grass. Grasswing reared, ready to trample the fallen stallion, but Rockwing kicked him from the ground, knocking his hooves out from under him. Grasswing crumbled. Rockwing staggered to his hooves and wiped the blood off his mouth with his wing. He circled Grasswing like a wolf, neck flat and low, teeth bared.

Silverlake glanced at Thunderwing. He and Jetfire

had abandoned their attack, and the mood of the watching steeds crackled like the sky before a lightning storm.

Grasswing heaved himself upright, but his back leg wouldn't hold him. He rolled to his other side and pulled himself to a slouching position. He faced Rockwing, ears pinned. The over-stallion spread his wings, blocking Silverlake's view, but she knew what was coming.

"Fly straight and find your rest," she whispered, and then she heard the blow that ended Grasswing's life. The battle was over.

Rockwing lifted off and hovered over his fallen foe. Silverlake saw Grasswing's golden hide and pale-green feathers spread flat on the field. His death was clean, he didn't suffer after the final strike, and he lay on his side with his eyes closed. He was in the golden meadow now with his colt, Graythorn, and all the others who had died today.

Silverlake glared at Rockwing, who was joined by several of his captains and the over-stallions from the other herds. Thunderwing conceded the battle and kneeled in surrender to prevent any more killing.

Rockwing waited for all the Sun Herd steeds to kneel before he spoke. "You have brought this on yourselves, Sun Herd," he said. "You lost the black foal, and in doing so you have endangered all of us. Even Snakewing is dead because of your actions." He gazed at Thunderwing.

Silverlake pricked her ears, glancing around Sky Meadow. Snakewing wasn't even here. What was he talking about?

"How is that?" asked Thunderwing.

"Snakewing and his warriors found the black foal hiding by the ocean in the Vein."

Silverlake couldn't hide her shocked gasp. They'd found Star!

"When they confronted him, the colt crushed Snakewing's skull." The Sun Herd steeds murmured fiercely. The last time they had seen Star he was a fragile weanling and not much of a fighter.

Rockwing paused dramatically. "And then your black foal called forth a beast from the sea to eat Snakewing while he was still alive."

"No!" screamed a pegasus in the distance.

Silverlake recognized her filly's voice with a sinking heart. Why wasn't Morningleaf hiding in the thicket?

"I don't believe it," Morningleaf continued.

Silverlake and the other pegasi shifted their eyes from Rockwing to the hollow in the grandmother tree.

"Bring the filly here," ordered Rockwing.

Two captains flew to the tree and yanked Morningleaf out of it with their teeth, gripping her by the roots of her wings. They flew her to Rockwing. Silverlake glimpsed the horrified look on her daughter's face.

"What do you know of the black foal?" asked Rockwing.

Silverlake tensed. Morningleaf looked small and fragile next to the thick Appaloosa stallion. "He's my friend," said her chestnut filly, eyes glowing. "I know he wouldn't kill anybody."

Rockwing threw back his head and whinnied. "The black foal has no friends." He looked at his captain, Frostfire. "This filly is loose minded, but maybe we can use her. Take her away."

Frostfire yanked Morningleaf aside and placed her under guard.

Silverlake's throat tightened until she could hardly breathe.

"This is what's going to happen," said Rockwing, addressing Thunderwing. "If the black foal is not delivered to me by his first birthday, your colts and all your stallions will be killed, and then I'll divide your mares, your fillies, and your lands between the four remaining herds."

Sun Herd hurled insults and curses at the dappled stallion.

Rockwing raised his wing. "If you don't like it, bring me the black foal. It's simple, really."

Rockwing placed Thunderwing under guard with Morningleaf. "It will be up to your mares to retrieve him, but not tonight. Tonight we celebrate."

In absolute misery, Sun Herd watched the conquering pegasi warriors celebrate their victory. A feast of crab apples was laid out, and the foreign warriors reenacted the day's battles with enthusiasm. Hundreds of dead bodies were dragged to the edges of Sky Meadow and stacked in large piles. The herds would have to depart in the morning before the stench of decay became too much to bear, and Sky Meadow would not be habitable for many years to come.

Silverlake stood outside Rockwing's camp and stared at her captured daughter. Her delicate red filly was curled up next to Thunderwing, and he had his bloody wing over her back. They each looked exhausted and overwhelmed by their failures—his to protect his herd and hers to obey her mother. Silent tears rolled from Silverlake's eyes as she seethed under the light of the Hundred Year Star. The approaching sound of hoofbeats startled her, and Silverlake whirled around. There stood Sweetroot, sweating, her wings shaking.

"I need your help," said the medicine mare. "Some of our steeds can still be saved."

Silverlake nodded, grateful to do something. She trotted behind Sweetroot to the willow tree where the injured Sun Herd steeds had gathered. As the conquering herds celebrated, Silverlake dug up roots with her hooves, gathered water, comforted orphaned foals, and focused her thoughts on surviving the night, since she had no idea what the morning would bring.

17

DELUSIONS

STAR WOKE TO AN EMPTY CAVE, HIS BODY
wracked by shivers.

"Crabwing!"

The silence that followed was absolute, and Star
remembered that his friend was dead. He lurched to
his hooves, drenched in sweat and sore all over. Blister-
ing pain ran from his jaws to his ears, his back leg was
inflamed, useless, and dried blood made his hide itch.

He limped out of his sea cave and trudged toward
the river. With every step he wanted to lie down and die.
He dragged his wings behind him out of habit, but then
the sight of his downtrodden shadow reminded him that
he wasn't a dud anymore—he could fly! It was the only

memory from yesterday that was good.

Star lifted off the beach from a standing position and cruised over the waves, letting the coastal breeze cool his body. The joy of flying sifted through his misery like sand falling through feathers, and he felt a pang of guilt for it.

He cruised over the bay to the river, and the fear of landing prickled his hide. Star tilted his wings and dropped, crashing into the river's bank and somersaulting into the water. Pain stabbed his wounded leg, and his head throbbed. He rested, letting the fresh water wash the blood off his hide and feathers. To his left was Crabwing's rock. It was picked clean of feathers and bones but was still red with blood. Star imagined Crabwing's bright face. "Fly straight and find your rest," he said.

When Star was clean, he climbed out of the river, hot and shivering at the same time. He watched the river for a long time and was surprised when it split suddenly into two rivers. How was that possible? He blinked, and the two rivers merged back into one.

Star closed his eyes, just for a second because he didn't want to fall asleep where the stinging fleas lived, but when he opened his eyes, he saw the sun had moved halfway across the sky. He wasn't safe here for reasons beyond the bugs. The Jungle Herd stallions would return for him with an army—it was time to move on.

He kicked off and soared over the cliffs to the dunes, taking a last look at the ocean. The gentle waves glittered under the sun, but the calm surface didn't fool Star. He knew what dangers lay beneath.

Several gulls dived into the waves, reminding him of Crabwing. Now that Star could fly, he was even more perplexed by Crabwing's choice to walk. "Good-bye, Crabwing," he said. Star angled inland and traveled southeast, leaving the ocean, the cave, and Snakewing's blood behind him.

He flew for two days, stopping often to rest. When he passed the same crooked oak tree twice, he realized he was flying in circles. Star landed smoothly in an open field and stared at the foreign landscape. He was lost.

Star squinted, trying to focus, and then yelped in surprise. Three pegasi circled above him. Morningleaf, Bumblewind, and Echofrost. "Hey there," he called, "I'm down here."

His friends circled closer, but they didn't speak. Star sat on his haunches for a rest. His hide was clammy, he'd lost all desire for food, and everything was a blur.

"We already passed this tree, didn't we, Morningleaf?" he asked the smallest of the three fliers, but Star's voice came out in a dry shriek. "Which way should we go now?"

Morningleaf pointed her wing south, and he noticed her feathers were so dull they looked brown. He wondered if she was sick. "Good plan. Just let me rest a minute." Star closed his eyes and fell onto his side.

He woke up later in a cold sweat, screaming. "Stop biting me!" Then he saw he was biting himself. He was trying to get rid of the flies that crawled over his open wounds, and his teeth had scraped off his fresh scab. Green pus mixed with blood oozed down his back leg.

The pain sharpened his vision for a moment, and he saw that the three pegasi were still circling him. "Why don't you come down here and help me?" he asked them. They didn't respond. *Maybe it's not Morningleaf, Bumblewind, and Echofrost,* he thought.

He staggered clumsily to his hooves. He had to keep moving. He didn't know what day it was or where he was, but he did know one thing: he needed a medicine mare.

Star flew out of the field, gaining altitude at a slow pace. In front of him he saw two giant redwood trees, like twins of each other, but they seemed to be floating. He flapped harder, trying to rise above them, but it was like he was flying backward. Star veered to avoid the tree on the right and nailed the one on the left headfirst.

He fluttered to the ground, his black feathers cascading around him, and landed with a grunt. He tried to get up, but it was impossible; his legs wouldn't obey his mind. The three pegasi circled lower, drawing ever closer. Star waved at them with his wing, hoping they would help him. The biggest one landed next to him. "Get Sweetroot of Sun Herd," he said. The creature leaned over him and hissed. Star blinked and saw it wasn't a pegasus at all; he was face-to-face with the bald, ugly head of a vulture.

"Uh-oh," he said, and then passed out just as the other two landed next to the first.

18

COUNTING THE DEAD

"OVER HERE," SAID SILVERLAKE TO DAWNFIR, HER voice low. "Get the others."

Silverlake fanned herself under the willow tree and waited. Soon Dawnfir returned with Hazelwind, Crystalfeather, Oakfire, and Sweetroot. Across the meadow, Mountain Herd, Jungle Herd, and Desert Herd celebrated their victory.

When everyone was present, Silverlake spoke. "Star was attacked by the Jungle Herd steeds near the cave where I hid him. I'm sure he's on the run now. We have to find him before anyone else does." She looked at each one of them. They were still stunned by the battle. Only her adult colt, Hazelwind, appeared alert, prancing, his body still coursing with excitement. He'd killed a fair number of warriors today in his first battle. With his arched neck and flickering muscles, he resembled his sire, Thunderwing.

Sweetroot put her wing on Hazelwind to settle him, but she spoke to all of them. "Can we take a moment for the dead?"

"Of course," said Silverlake.

They dropped their heads as Sweetroot spoke the names of the fallen. Her mind was sharp from memorizing herbs and remedies, and she was able to list several hundred pegasi by name and family of origin. She finished with the three supporters of Star who had died: Ashfire, Violetsun, and Grasswing.

"Fallen pegasi of Sun Herd," she said, "you served us with your lives, and there is no greater honor. As your bodies return to dust, we know you live forever in the golden meadow, where pain cannot follow you and where death has been conquered. Fly straight and find your rest."

"Fly straight and find your rest," the gathered steeds repeated.

"I'm going to ask permission to look for Star," Silverlake said. "Does anyone want to go with me?"

"I can't leave," said Sweetroot. She had gathered all

the wounded Sun Herd pegasi in one area where she could treat them and bring them water. Silverlake had seen medicine mares from the other four herds doing the same for their injured. Every herd had paid a steep price today.

Crystalfeather folded her wings. "I can't leave either, not until I find out what happened to Echofrost." Now that they were all Rockwing's captives, Crystalfeather hoped to be reunited with her abducted filly.

Silverlake nodded. While she was spying on Mountain Herd, she'd witnessed horrible treatment of Echofrost. The filly was bullied and brutalized by the weanlings and yearlings of the herd. They wouldn't let her sleep or graze. They bit her tail and ripped out most of the hair. Bracken-tail, however, had received much better treatment. He was still glossy and well fed. In fact, it seemed that Rockwing was protecting the brown colt. Silverlake could not even guess why he would do that.

"What do you make of Rockwing's story?" asked Oak-fire. "About Star killing Snakewing and controlling the animals in the sea?"

The pegasi stood in silence, swishing their tails. "It doesn't sound like Star," Dawnfir finally said.

"Maybe he *is* the destroyer," Hazelwind said quietly.

"Impossible," said Crystalfeather, stamping her hoof.

"Why impossible?" asked Hazelwind, still pumped from battle in spite of Sweetroot's attempt to calm him.

"Because they didn't all die for the sake of a destroyer." Crystalfeather waved her wing over the piles of dead Sun Herd pegasi. Her eyes were black and unreadable, her words strangled. "And we didn't abandon my filly to Mountain Herd savages for the sake of a destroyer." She glared at Hazelwind. "We can't be wrong."

Silverlake saw her colt calm down, rebuked, but Hazelwind added, "Well, Rockwing wasn't lying. I heard the Jungle Herd warriors talking about it, and their fear is real. They saw Star kill Snakewing with an over-stallion's deathblow, and then a sea creature he'd been swimming with earlier came to the shore and took Snakewing underwater in its jaws without touching Star, who was standing right there." Hazelwind's eyes brightened with the excitement of the tale.

Silverlake held up her wing. "Stories, especially those told by scared pegasi who'd failed their mission and got their over-stallion killed, get exaggerated. Who knows what really happened?" She swept her eyes over all of them. "I do agree that Rockwing wasn't lying—Snakewing is dead and Star was there when it happened, but that doesn't mean he's the destroyer."

Hazelwind looked up at the Hundred Year Star, and the others followed his gaze. It was bigger, brighter, and growing every day—a constant reminder that the final hours were near.

Silverlake chewed her lip. Only one black foal in history, Nightwing, had ever lived this long, and he had been a disaster. She arched her neck against her own doubts. "We know the risk we've taken," she said, more to herself than to the others. "Of course it's possible that Star's a destroyer."

Dawnfir lashed her tail. "Lightfeather was my best friend. I watched Sun Herd abandon her when she was pregnant. I watched her fly through a lightning storm. I watched her give birth to a dead foal and then bring him back to life. I watched her love him until she took her last breath, and then I watched her die." Dawnfir sobbed into her wings and then glared at each gathered steed, not with accusation, but with conviction. "She was never angry with Sun Herd for abandoning her. She understood our fear, but I don't believe she went through all that for the destroyer."

Silverlake nodded. "That is our hope, Dawnfir, and so we need to find him before Rockwing does. Will you go with me to look for him?"

"I will."

Silverlake nodded, determined, and then glanced around. Rockwing and the three other over-stallions were guarding the sky and the land all around them. Escaping to search for the black foal was impossible. "We won't be able to leave without Rockwing's permission."

"He'll say no to you," said Dawnfir, her wings sagging. "You're the one who hid Star."

"Actually, I don't think he will," said Silverlake, rubbing her feathers against her weary eyes. "I have an idea."

19

THE DREAM

MORNINGLEAF FLEW OVER SKY MEADOW ASSESS-
ing the damage to the herd. She counted the bodies of the
living and the dead, keeping track of the numbers in her
head. Later she would make a report to her father. She
circled for a long time, and two mares circled with her:
Silverlake and Dawnfir.

"Look at that black pegasus," Dawnfir said, nodding
downward.

Morningleaf followed her gaze, and sure enough, a
black steed was crumpled on the grass in a heap, covered
in flies. "It must be Star," said Morningleaf, but Star was
living in a cave, wasn't he?

She landed next to the stallion and saw a festering

*wound on his flank. It reeked of infection. "Get Sweetroot,"
she said, and Silverlake flew away. "Star?" she said to the
black steed.*

*He didn't move, and his forehead was solid black. It
couldn't be Star. "Who are you?" Morningleaf pushed his
body with her wing. The movement caused the wound to
drip pus onto the grass, and where it landed, the grass
died and black flowers sprung out of the soil. She shoved
the stallion again. "Get up."*

*He startled and swiveled his head at her, teeth bared.
Silver starfire electrified his hide, and smoke drifted from
his nostrils. "You want to know who I am?" he asked,
spraying the grass with sparks. "I'm the destroyer."*

*Morningleaf screamed, and a hoof as hard as bedrock
snapped her neck.*

*"Where's Star?" she said, falling and landing on a bed
of her own blue feathers.*

Nightwing snorted. "I ate him."

Morningleaf woke from her dream in a cold sweat.
Thunderwing was up and consulting his captains. Her
eyes swept Sun Herd's grasslands with renewed horror.
The dead were piled along the boundaries of Sky Meadow.
The wounded were groaning under Sweetroot's care. The
stench of death and infection permeated the air. Shocked

steeds wandered aimlessly, unable to graze because of the blood and fluid on the grass, and weanlings bleated like newborn foals. Flamesky, who had lost both her parents, stood with Crystalfeather, but her eyes were blank and reflective, like the surface of Big Sky Lake.

Morningleaf wanted to go back to sleep, but the memory of her dream was too vivid. What did it mean? Was Nightwing returning or was Star going to be a destroyer? Her thoughts chilled her, and she remembered the oozing wound. Star was in trouble, only of that was she certain.

She scanned the meadow for her mother and spotted her speaking with Star's supporters. Then Silverlake and Dawnfir separated and flew over the grass, landing near the over-stallions—Rockwing, Icewing, Sandwing, and Jungle Herd's new over-stallion, Smokewing. While the mares waited to be addressed, Morningleaf trotted to the edge of her boundary to listen.

Rockwing finally looked at them. "You may speak."

"We seek your permission to search for the black foal," said Silverlake.

Another group of mares led by Brackentail's dam, Rowanwood, appeared. "Don't let her go," Rowanwood said. "She nursed the black foal. She just wants to help him."

Rockwing braced at Rowanwood's commanding tone but listened. "Is that true?" he asked Silverlake.

"Yes," Silverlake said matter-of-factly.

"Then how can I trust you to bring him back if you find him?"

Silverlake looked directly at Morningleaf, and Morningleaf saw sorrow buried beneath her mother's fear. "Because you have my filly."

Rockwing snorted. "So *you* are Silverlake, the banished lead mare of Sun Herd?"

Silverlake nodded.

"And this is your filly?" Rockwing pointed his wing at Morningleaf.

Morningleaf saw her mother's knees quiver as she nodded agreement.

"She's pretty," he said.

An avalanche of fury crashed behind her mother's unblinking stare, but only a slight trembling of her silver feathers belied her feelings.

Morningleaf whispered to Thunderwing in awe, "Look how strong she is. She wants to strike him, but she's as still as a viper."

Thunderwing exhaled, his eyes riveted on Silverlake. "Indeed. She's always been a steadfast mare."

"The black foal trusts me," Silverlake said. "I will bring him to you and trade him for my filly's freedom."

Morningleaf opened her mouth to protest, and Thunderwing slapped his wing over her mouth. "Shh," he nickered.

Rockwing furrowed his brow, thinking for some time, and then he spoke to everyone. "I believe Silverlake is properly motivated to return the black foal to me." He looked at Silverlake. "If you return him before midnight on his birthday, the filly may choose her own herd. If you're late, the filly dies."

Silverlake gasped. "But—"

"That's the deal; take it or leave it."

Silverlake blinked at him, unable to speak, and then she looked at Morningleaf. They both knew she had no intention of bringing Star back before his birthday. Silverlake had tried to trick Rockwing but had instead fallen into a trap. Morningleaf would die when Silverlake failed to return. But Morningleaf was prepared to accept that fate. She folded her aqua wings and nodded to her mother.

Silverlake, fierce with pride, nodded back, and then turned and glared at Rockwing. "We have a deal."

Morningleaf's knees buckled, and she sank to the grass, proud of her mother. A good lead mare did what was best for the whole herd, not just for her own filly. And Morningleaf's mother, banished or not, was a good lead mare. "I knew I would never see Dawn Meadow again," Morningleaf nickered to herself, thinking of the next migration.

"What did you say?" asked Thunderwing.

Morningleaf exhaled. "Nothing. It's not important."

Rowanwood whinnied. "We still want to go," she said, indicating her group. "And if I find the black foal, can I trade him for my colt, Brackentail?"

Rockwing pinned his ears. "Brackentail?"

"Yes, you captured him in the canyons." Rowanwood's voice faltered. "He's still alive, isn't he?"

Rockwing snorted. "You mean Brackentail the Betrayer? Yes. He's alive. He helped me plan this little attack." Rockwing circled his wing over the stacks of dead bodies bordering Sky Meadow.

"No!" Rowanwood sucked in her breath. "He couldn't have done that!"

Beside Morningleaf, her father flared his wings, and Rockwing's guards rushed forward to subdue him. "No," said Thunderwing, but in a tone that reminded her of her dream. Nearby, the Sun Herd steeds vibrated their wings in rage.

Rockwing looked pleased. "Brackentail hates the black foal as much as you do. After he failed to kill him in the canyons, he made a deal with me." Rockwing smirked at Thunderwing. "Brackentail the Betrayer is one of us now."

Rowanwood lunged to attack Rockwing, but his captains flew in her way. "It's not true!" she said.

"Take her away," said Rockwing.

"Wait!" she cried, and swept her wing over the destruction of Sun Herd. "All of this is the black foal's fault—and I don't trust her." She glared at Silverlake. "Please let me and my mares search too. Between Silverlake's group and mine, one of us is sure to find the black foal."

Rockwing assessed the two groups. "I believe you are also properly motivated to return the foal to me, Rowanwood. I grant you permission to leave."

Rowanwood whirled around, and her group kicked off immediately. Several more angry mares assembled, and they also received permission to search for Star.

Silverlake stalled her departure, and Morningleaf wasn't sure why until her mother found a moment to speak to her. "Are you hurt, Morningleaf?" she whispered.

"I'm fine, but I think something is wrong with Star. He needs you."

"We're leaving now; we'll find him."

"Just you two?" Morningleaf asked, looking at Dawnfir. Silverlake nodded.

"No, Mother, I saw Star in my dream; he's hurt. You need to bring a medicine mare with you."

Silverlake glanced at the hundreds of wounded warriors. "Sweetroot and her apprentices are too busy to leave."

"Mama, look around. What was all this for if it wasn't to keep him alive? We can't quit now; and if you go without help, you'll only watch him die. Rockwing will kill our stallions and scatter the rest of us. It means the end of Sun Herd forever. You have to convince Sweetroot."

Tears welled in her mother's eyes, and she nodded.

"And Mama, don't trade Star to save me. Please."

Silverlake wrapped her wings around Morningleaf, pulling her to her chest and choking on her sobs. Then she trotted away with Dawnfir to find Sweetroot. The sun was rising in the sky, and the other search parties had left. Silverlake's group had to find him first or all was lost.

Morningleaf closed her eyes and sent good thoughts to Star. *Hold on; help is on the way.*

When she opened her eyes, she saw Silverlake, Dawnfir, and Sweetroot flying into the clouds.

20

THREE HUNGRY BIRDS

STAR'S EYES FLEW OPEN. "ACK!" HIS FLANK FELT like it was on fire. He lurched upward, scrambling to get his hooves under him, and then he sank back into the weeds feeling faint. Something was stinging or biting him. He strained to get a better view of his leg, panting and flailing his wings, but he saw nothing.

Then he felt it again, and this time he glimpsed his tormentor. It was a vulture. He raised his head and saw the stinky bird pecking at his open wound. Star gagged, and the field spun around him. Another vulture flapped its wings in Star's face, and a third circled above him. He jolted out of his stupor. He wouldn't die this way. He kicked the vulture with his good leg, knocking the creature back.

It hissed like an angry goose.

Star shook his head. He was going crazy out here in the Vein. Where were Morningleaf, Bumblewind, and Echofrost?

His body was burning hot, but he was shivering. It was early evening, and he couldn't remember the last time he'd eaten or drank. The other vulture landed, and the three of them faced him, big and bald. He swiped at them with his long wings, and they jumped back, exchanging hissing noises.

Star forced himself to his hooves. If this was his last battle, he'd fight it standing up. He whinnied, amazed that he wouldn't be assassinated by an over-stallion, he wouldn't receive his power from the Hundred Year Star, and he wouldn't heal or destroy the herds—he would die in a final battle against three hungry birds, and after he died there would be nothing left of him but bones.

"He has plenty of life left in him," said one of the birds. Oh no, they were talking. Star blinked, sure he'd gone mad.

"We have to hide him before the others find us."

Star peered at the sky. Were more vultures coming?

"Let's herd him." The three birds opened their wings and tried to herd him like a horse toward the woods.

"You think I can't hear you?" he said to them. He opened his wings and flew away from them, but they followed, flying beside him.

"Star, please land," said one of them, sounding like Silvercloud.

The world blurred, and Star watched the ground rush toward him. *How did that get there?* And then he crashed into it. A scream erupted unbidden from the depths of his chest when he landed on his swollen flank. The vultures landed, and one fanned him with its wings while another stroked his tense neck. "How do you know my name?" he asked them.

"It's me, Silvercloud, now Silverlake."

"But you're a vulture," he said.

She brushed his forelock out of his eyes. "There were vultures here, Star, but we chased them away. You're sick."

Well, that was true. "You look like a vulture."

Silverlake snorted. "No, Star, it's me and Dawnfir, and Sweetroot."

"Sweetroot," he whispered, "what's wrong with me?"

Then he heard her comforting voice. "You have a serious infection, and I can help you, but first I need you to walk to those redwood trees where no one will spot you from the sky."

"Is this a trick?" he asked.

"Well, if it were, would I tell you?" Sweetroot scolded. "You're going to have to trust me and get moving. You're too big to carry."

Star obeyed; he had no other choice. They looked like big vultures to him, but they sounded like his friends. He let them herd him into the dense forest. As soon as he was under the cover of the trees, he lay down. Sweetroot went to work right away. "I have to drain this wound, Star. It's going to hurt."

He nodded.

"Bite this." She offered him a piece of bark. "There are a lot of pegasi out searching for you; we can't be discovered, so be as quiet as you can." Sweetroot bent over his flank and sliced the wound open with her teeth. Star clenched and bit the bark in half, tears pouring from his eyes and sweat dripping off his hide. The old mare squeezed the wound, and a gooey mixture of greenish pus and red blood shot out and splattered a tree.

And for Star, everything faded to black.

When he woke, it was dark. Dawnfir was huddled against his back, warming him with her body. His fever had broken, and he could see clearly. "You're not vultures," he nickered with relief.

The mares whinnied, amused. "Drink this," said Sweetroot, holding out her cupped, watertight wings. "It will control the infection and reduce your pain."

Star drank the pungent water treated with herbs. He noticed that a poultice of leaves and chewed roots had been packed into his festering wound.

"What about my leg? I think I broke it."

"No. It's bruised and swollen, but it will heal. You're going to be fine, Star."

Silverlake stood guard over the group, and Star relaxed. They spent the evening in silence. Star sensed that they had bad news, but he was in no hurry to hear it. He would rest before he asked about the captured weanlings and the fresh battle wounds he noticed on the mares.

The next day they brought Star water, late-blooming crab apples, and more medicine. He hobbled on his hooves and grazed. "You've grown a lot since I last saw you," said Silverlake.

Star nodded, remembering. When he and Silverlake had crossed the Drink, he'd been smaller than she, still on the long-legged side, and unable to fly.

"How do you feel?" she asked him.

"Better."

The four of them grazed near a bubbling forest creek. It was time to talk. Silverlake gave the worst news first. "Rockwing joined with the other herds, and they attacked us two days ago. We lost."

Anger flared in Star's heart. "Where's Morningleaf?" he asked. "Was she hurt?"

Silverlake sighed. "She's alive but captured, along with Thunderwing and the rest. I was banished for hiding you from Sun Herd, but I came back for the battle." She paused. "But, Star, Grasswing is dead."

Star crumpled. "No."

Dawnfir spoke. "He went against Rockwing in a stand-off. His death ended the battle. We—we weren't winning anyway. Grasswing saved many lives with what he did, and he gave Rockwing wounds he'll have scars from forever. He will never forget this fight."

"Grasswing is a legend now," said Sweetroot. "Like your mother."

Star hardened himself against the grief that threatened to overwhelm him. Grasswing had been like a sire to him. He swallowed his anger so he could focus on Morningleaf and his friends. "Where is Sun Herd now?"

Silverlake answered, "The battle happened in Sky Meadow, but because of all the . . . blood . . . Rockwing has probably moved them all to his territory by now."

Star saw her brace herself against the memory. "How did you escape him?"

"We didn't," said Silverlake. "He let us go to bring you back, and we will, but not until after you receive your power."

Dawnfir sighed. "That's right; if you go too soon, Rockwing will kill you, or try to force a pact with you." She glanced at Silverlake. "He's cruel."

Star sighed. "So what's your plan?"

"We'll hide here until your birthday. After you receive the fire from the Hundred Year Star, we'll rescue Sun Herd, and everyone else he's captured," said Silverlake. "One way or another, this will be over."

Star didn't miss the implication in her words "one way or another." Silverlake still had doubts about him, and he couldn't blame her. He remembered the forest fire, Echofrost's capture, Crabwing, and the sea creature that snatched Snakewing in its jaws—Star attracted destruction, and yet he lived. Malformed, motherless, unable to fly, marked for execution, and mortally wounded—he had rebounded from all of it. It appeared he would fulfill his destiny as Silverlake predicted—for better or for worse.

"Okay," he agreed, "we'll wait."

21

THE BARGAIN

STAR WOKE ON THE MORNING OF HIS FIRST birthday feeling excited and sick. Today he would receive the starfire. He stretched in the hollow of the redwood tree where the four of them had been hiding the last two days. His hoof scraped against Sweetroot's side.

"Watch it," she snapped, her eyes still closed.

His other leg kicked Dawnfir in the belly.

"Ugh," she grunted.

Silverlake opened her eyes. It was dawn, and soft light lit up the floating dust and webs all around them. "If you can't sleep, go outside," she said.

Star emerged from the tree cave and stretched properly. He felt much better after two days of rest and Sweetroot's medicine. The swelling in his flank was almost gone, his infection was cured, and a thin scab covered his wound. His belly was full from feasting on fallen nuts, berries, and the last of the season's crab apples. He preened his shiny black feathers.

Silverlake popped out of the tree and approached him. "So you can fly now?"

A swift breeze tousled his mane. "I can." Silverlake paused, and he felt she wanted to say more. "What is it?" he asked.

Silverlake blew softly. "What really happened to Snakewing?"

A vision of Snakewing in the jaws of the orca sent his heart racing, and he shook away the awful memory. "I can't talk about it."

Silverlake stood next to him for a long time before she spoke. "A pegasus's first kill is his hardest."

"So it gets easier?"

"Much."

"Why doesn't that make me feel any better?" Star studied the bark on the redwood tree, wondering what was wrong with him. Why was he so different from all the rest? "I don't want to kill pegasi."

Silverlake nodded. "That's probably a good thing in

your case," she said, folding her wings. "Don't lose your hope."

Star looked at her and saw his face reflected in her dark eyes. "What if I am the destroyer?"

Silverlake swiveled her ears, always listening for patrols. "Maybe it will be your choice what you are."

"Maybe it won't."

Silverlake swished her tail and knocked a bee out of the sky that had flown too close to her. "We're seeing this through, Star." She lifted her chin the way Morningleaf did when her mind was made up.

"At any cost?" Star asked.

Silverlake arched her neck. "I don't know, but I can promise you this—if you're not the healer, I will break my wings and run myself off a cliff."

Her fierce expression made Star chuckle. "I know of a nice steep one on the coast," he said, thinking of the cliff he'd fallen off the day he learned to fly.

She softened, nickering with him, and he realized she didn't know what was going to happen next any more than he did. Star flicked his ears, suddenly uncomfortable. "But why are you so certain of me?"

Silverlake took a deep breath, her eyes far away and glistening with tears she refused to shed. "Because your mother was certain." She trotted away to join Sweetroot.

Star's gut was in turmoil the rest of the day as he waited for dusk. At midnight the Hundred Year Star would transfer its fire to him. What would it feel like? Would it transform him into a killer? His nerves tingled, and he spooked at every noise, driving the mares crazy.

As soon as it was dusk, Star whistled for Silverlake. "I can't wait until midnight. Let's go now."

Silverlake's eyes widened. "No, we have to wait until after midnight."

"You said you had a hiding place where you spied on Mountain Herd. Take me there. I need to see Sun Herd and Morningleaf while I'm . . . still me."

Sweetroot shook her head. "If you're captured before midnight, you could be killed, and then the war and everything will be for nothing."

He stood taller. "I won't be captured. I can fly and I can fight, but I can't wait a moment longer." Star's muscles quivered with agitation.

The three mares exchanged terrified glances, but Star didn't back down. Finally Silverlake agreed. "Okay, I'll take you to my hiding spot."

Star closed his eyes and took a deep breath, smelling the warm bark, listening to the calls of the cardinals, and feeling the rays of the setting sun on his feathers. These were his last hours as a weanling.

"Ready?" Silverlake asked the group.

"Ready," they said, and Silverlake kicked off into the darkening sky. "Stay close to me," she warned.

Star galloped into the sky, his heart lifting with the thrill of flight. He flattened his neck and soared, easily catching the mares.

"Look at you," Sweetroot said. "You've become quite the young stallion."

Star beamed. He wasn't even close to full grown.

Silverlake guided them, flying fast and low, their hooves brushing the treetops. Ahead of them loomed the Blue Mountains.

Star overheard Sweetroot's words to Silverlake. "I hope we're not too late," she said.

"Too late for what?" Star asked.

Silverlake's expression went blank, and she changed the subject. "Look, there's Sky Meadow."

Star tensed. The mares had told him all about the battle, but he wasn't prepared to see the piles of bodies stacked along the edges of the meadow. The bodies showed the marks of wolves and bears. Blood and broken feathers smeared the grass where not long ago he'd played chase with his friends. A wave of nausea rolled through him. He spotted a splash of green feathers on a palomino hide, and he faltered, almost falling from the sky. It was Grasswing. "Oh no," Star whispered.

"Don't look," said Silverlake.

Star averted his eyes and blinked rapidly to clear his vision, but his hot tears fell on Sky Meadow like rain, and his chest quaked with his silent sobs. He didn't want to remember Sun Herd or Grasswing this way.

"They're in the golden meadow," Sweetroot whispered.

Star flew on, and behind him an embarrassing trail of white flowers sprang up where his tears had fallen. Silverlake had always been impressed by the flowers, calling them magical, but they just made Star feel all the more different and cursed.

He blinked and focused on the Blue Mountains ahead, letting anger replace his misgivings.

They reached the mountain range. "Where to?" asked Dawnfir.

Silverlake angled her wings, losing altitude. "We'll go the rest of the way on hoof," she said.

The four of them landed at the base of the ridge leading to Silverlake's lookout. Star tested his legs on the steep, rocky terrain. His stifle joint under his flank ached, but he could climb. He followed the mares, scrambling up the narrow path to the plateau. A quick glance at the position of the moon in the sky told him it was almost midnight.

Star pulled himself over the ridge and halted next to the mares. They scooted aside to let him look. Spread below was Rockwing's Canyon Meadow. It was well lit by the Hundred Year Star, which washed the huge canyon in yellow tones almost as bright as the sun. Star saw thousands of steeds making up Rockwing's army, the warriors from the other herds, all of Mountain Herd, and the survivors of Sun Herd. They couldn't all fit in the canyon and so they overflowed into the surrounding valleys.

Sun Herd was easy to spot. They had been corralled into the center and were guarded by thick-legged Mountain Herd stallions. In contrast to the other herds, the Sun Herd pegasi were the most colorful and the most depressed. They huddled together, wings tucked, and stared blankly at the Hundred Year Star, waiting. Star's breath hitched at the forlorn sight of his once proud herd.

He scanned the meadow for Rockwing. There was an outcropping of flat rock that created a natural pedestal at one end of the wide canyon. There he spotted the five overstallions of the five herds: Rockwing, Sandwing, Icewing, Smokewing, and Thunderwing. Several captains flanked them, and in the center a lone chestnut filly reared defiantly under their watchful eyes: Morningleaf.

Star's gut dropped like a stone in a river. "Why is Morningleaf on the rock with the over-stallions?" The rest of Sun Herd's captives, including Echofrost, waited on the grass.

Silverlake said nothing.

Star faced her. Her silver feathers looked gold in the light, and he was briefly reminded of how his mother had looked before she died. "What have you done?" he demanded.

Silverlake's voice quivered. "I had to do it, Star."

"Do what?" But Star could guess what. "Did you trade her so you could come looking for me?" Star arched to his full height, towering over Silverlake and thrusting his chest at her, his mind reeling.

Silverlake lowered her head in submission. "Maybe I made a mistake."

He bellowed at her. "Maybe?"

Dawnfir pushed between them. "Rockwing didn't leave Silverlake a choice," she said, trying to calm him down. "She had to trade Morningleaf for the chance to look for you. With all the search parties, it was the only way to make sure we found you first."

Star lashed his tail, unmoved.

Dawnfir continued, "And it's a good thing we did, because vultures were circling you and you were dying from your wounds. If the other mares had found you, they would have finished you off and been done with it—and all of us, *including Morningleaf*, would be lost."

Star flattened his ears. "What was the bargain?"

Dawnfir glanced at Silverlake and then answered. "If Silverlake doesn't deliver you before midnight tonight, Rockwing will kill Morningleaf."

Fresh bewilderment subdued Star's rage. "Why her?"

"Because Morningleaf stood up for you after the battle, and Rockwing captured her. He found out who she was, and then Silverlake made the deal."

"A deal you have no intention of honoring," he said, glancing at Silverlake.

"It was the only way to keep you alive," she said.

Star shook his head, stunned. "You're willing to sacrifice Morningleaf . . . for me?"

Silverlake threw up her wings. "Yes. And Morningleaf agrees."

In frustration, Morningleaf's words flew out of Star's mouth. "You don't fight a pegasus on the terms he sets. You will always lose," he added.

Silverlake choked back her sudden sobs. "I'm sorry."

Sweetroot touched Star's wing. "It's easy to second guess Silverlake from up here on the rock, Star." She swept her wings over the vast meadow full of pegasi below them. "We did the best we could. You're alive, aren't you? And so is Morningleaf for now, so stop grumbling and do something."

Star followed her eyes and gazed at the assembled steeds in the canyon valleys. Morningleaf stood with her chin set and her ears pinned while Rockwing spoke to her. There wasn't a hint of fear in the filly, and her bravery crushed Star's heart.

Sweetroot had spoken the truth. He wasn't there when Rockwing conquered Sun Herd, so it was wrong of him to judge his adoptive mother.

"I understand why you did it," he said to Silverlake. "You're a lead mare. It's your duty to protect the entire herd."

"That's right," she said with a sigh.

Star spread his mighty wings. "But it's not my duty." With that, he galloped forward and dived off the plateau.

22

PROMISES

"NO!" SCREAMED SILVERLAKE, AND SHE LEAPED off the plateau behind him, followed by Sweetroot and Dawnfir.

Star pulled out of his dive and cruised over the assembled herds in a wide circle. His shadow darkened the meadow, causing the gathered steeds to look up. Screams erupted from the surprised pegasi, and they stampeded like horses, by hoof, afraid of the open sky where he flew.

"It's the destroyer!"

"Nightwing has returned."

The pegasi ducked and covered their heads, waiting for Nightwing's fire.

Star felt the same fear, and he looked behind him

for Nightwing, until he realized they were talking about him. Didn't they notice the white star on his forehead? He tucked his wings and flew faster, scattering pegasi in his wake.

"Wait, it's not time!" Silverlake neighed after him.

Star ignored her. With five over-stallions thirsting for his blood, he doubted he would survive the hour, but he didn't care. He was just in time to save Morningleaf.

He landed in front of the over-stallions, taller than three of them. Silverlake and the mares landed beside him.

Morningleaf rushed to his side and nuzzled his neck.

The pegasi in the canyons halted their stampede and watched, trembling and confused.

Morningleaf craned her neck to look at him, her eyes swelling with tears of relief. "You've grown," she said.

He nickered. "No. You've shrunk."

With chaos all around them, Star and Morningleaf saw only each other.

Silverlake let out her breath. "It's all up to them now," she said to Sweetroot and Dawnfir.

A white stallion with one blue eye rushed forward and snatched Morningleaf's wing in his jaws. Star recognized Frostfire, the Mountain Herd stallion who had kidnapped him seven moons ago.

Star grabbed her other wing, but when Frostfire tugged her away and Morningleaf squealed in pain, Star let her go, rage blackening his thoughts. He turned and faced Rockwing. "I'm here. You can release her."

"Have you come to accept my deal?" Rockwing asked, referring to the pact he hoped to make with Star.

"What deal?" asked Morningleaf, exasperated and grimacing as Frostfire sank his teeth deeper into her ruffled aqua feathers.

Star ignored her. "No. I'm here to honor Silverlake's promise. I believe she offered my life for Morningleaf's."

"No, Star. Please, don't do it," cried Morningleaf.

Rockwing fidgeted. Star doubted he'd prepared for such a quick and easy surrender. Rockwing glanced at the Hundred Year Star, and Star followed his gaze. It pulsed, growing larger by the minute. Rockwing spoke. "It's not too late to make a pact with me, black foal. Save your life and bring peace to Anok."

The other four over-stallions grumbled, shifting their hooves in confusion. The pegasi in the meadow listened, their ears swiveling to catch every word.

Star pinned his ears. "No. You promised Morningleaf's life for mine, and that is the pact I've come to fulfill."

A bird sang, a long, low whistle, tricked by the light of the Hundred Year Star into thinking it was day. Rockwing pricked his ears at the sound and then agreed. "Okay, I accept." He caught the eye of Frostfire. "Let her go."

Frostfire dropped Morningleaf's wing and pushed her with his muzzle, urging her to fly off the flat outcropping of rock on which they all stood.

"Go," said Silverlake, also nudging her filly.

"I won't go," Morningleaf neighed, and then she flattened her neck and rammed Star like a mountain goat. "Fly away, Star; it's almost midnight!"

Star didn't budge, and his heart melted when she looked at him, confusion and fear flickering in her amber eyes.

"Please," she said.

Sadness blanketed Star. Soon he would be dead, and the herds would fight for another hundred years, and then they would execute the next black foal like they were about to do him. It was a cycle that would never end. He turned his back on Rockwing, and he faced the gathered steeds below the rocky plateau.

"Look where we are," he said, his voice booming, quieting even the crickets. His authority fell on the pegasi like folded wings, grounding them. "And for what?" he asked, looking at individual steeds as he spoke. "How does breaking us make us whole?" He paused, waiting for an answer. None came.

He turned to Rockwing. "Take my life for Morningleaf's and be done with it."

"No," Morningleaf whinnied, choking on tears. Silverlake wrapped her chestnut filly in her wings.

Star kneeled before Rockwing and lowered his head for execution.

Rockwing snorted. "We could have ruled Anok together, black foal, you and me. What have you gained by denying me? Nothing but death." He tucked his wings. "I won't take your bad luck upon myself." Rockwing indicated the big bay stallion to his left. "Thunderwing will do the honors."

It had always been Thunderwing's duty to execute Star, and the crimson-feathered over-stallion didn't look surprised by Rockwing's request. Thunderwing stepped forward.

"Father, no," begged Morningleaf as her mother dragged her away. Then Morningleaf looked at Star. "Please! If you let them do this to you, I'll hate you forever." She sniffled and her wings vibrated, shedding downy aqua feathers all around her.

Star opened his eyes and stared into hers. If the pegasi in Anok were more like her, they wouldn't need a healer because they wouldn't be so broken in the first place. He swept his black feathers over her cheek. "No, you won't."

Monringleaf gasped.

Star tucked his wings and faced Thunderwing. "I'm ready."

Thunderwing steeled himself, examining Star for the best placement of the blow. The pegasi in the meadow stood as still as stones.

When he was ready, Thunderwing reared, using his wide wings to steady himself.

Star braced. For all his fears, he hadn't really thought it would end this way. But he should have known. Thunderwing had promised this very thing on the day he was born. But Morningleaf was safe. She would live on.

Thunderwing pinned his ears, and without any more hesitation, he dropped his sharpened front hoof in the over-stallion's death strike.

23

MIDNIGHT

STAR HEARD THE CRUSH OF HOOF AGAINST BONE, but he felt nothing. *I'm dead*, he thought, but then the lone bird whistled again. Star raised his head and saw the shocked expression of Thunderwing.

A flurry of feathers rained between them. Star blinked, more confused than ever. But then he saw that the feathers were blue, and his heart skidded to a halt. His eyes followed the path of the falling feathers in time to see a chestnut filly with a flaxen mane and tail tumble across the rocks and fall head over tail off the plateau. Star's thoughts shattered as he realized what had just happened: Morningleaf had flown into the path of Thunderwing's hoof and had taken the blow meant for Star.

Time raced forward, and Star flew to the filly just as she crashed onto the grass. Morningleaf landed in a crumbled heap; her right wing was snapped in half, and droplets of blood splattered her feathers. But it was the sight of Morningleaf's neck that caused the canyon meadow to spin for Star. It was broken, and her head was twisted and impossibly facing the wrong way. Her small body twitched as if it had been struck by lightning.

"Morningleaf?" Star cried, gently rubbing her shoulder with his wing.

She blinked at him, squinting like he was far, far away.

Silverlake and Sweetroot landed next to them. Silverlake couldn't speak. Sweetroot quietly and swiftly inspected the injuries.

Morningleaf wrinkled her brow. "I can't get up."

"Shh," said Silverlake. "Don't try."

Morningleaf rolled her eyes to look at Star. "You can't win when they set the terms, Star. Remember?"

Star's thoughts collided in rage and grief. He couldn't answer.

Silverlake laid her head next to her filly and sobbed.

"Don't be sad, Mama. Look over there; I see Grasswing."

Silverlake looked and then shook her head. "No, sweet

filly, I don't see him."

Echofrost and Bumblewind forced their way through the crowd and settled next to Morningleaf. "We're here," said Echofrost.

Morningleaf wheezed, straining to breathe while the light in her amber eyes began to fade. "Good," she said.

Star wiped his eyes, his tears falling freely, and then he saw the spirits, like colorful lights. It was Grasswing and Lightfeather. They flew down from the night sky, landed, and leaned over Morningleaf. Star blinked, looking around him, but none of the gathered steeds appeared to notice the spirits. Star wondered how he could see them. In so many ways, he was not a regular pegasus.

"Lightfeather!" Morningleaf said with delight.

"No, no," cried Silverlake, dropping to her knees and looking blankly past the spirits at the stars above. "Please don't take her."

Star blinked, blinded by the glowing presence of Lightfeather and Grasswing, and then the spirit of Morningleaf rose from her injured body. Her blue feathers shimmered with light, and her head twisted around until it was once again properly aligned with her neck.

Star felt like he was floating, like there was nothing left in Anok to hold him in place, to give him purpose, like he could blow away with the wind.

Lightfeather touched noses with Morningleaf and then she looked at Star. His mother's unfathomable eyes pierced his mind, and it was the opposite of floating—it was like she'd pushed him off a cliff. He fell into the past, bouncing off memories as he dropped into a deep, black canyon—he saw Crabwing gulping oysters, the twins playing chase, Brackentail jeering at him, Thunderwing striking the ground, Mossberry telling stories, and then he saw himself, a long-legged colt unable to fly.

The speed of his descent made him dizzy until he reached the night he was born, and then his brain jolted to a halt. He saw Lightfeather lying in her grove with him; his tongue was blue and his eyes were closed. He watched like it was happening now in front of him. Lightfeather massaged his chest with her wingtips, but nothing happened. She grew frantic, and then she bit his ear, and the pain slammed him back into his body where he took his first breath.

Star flashed forward a few hours, and there was Lightfeather whispering secrets into his ears until the very last minute. Her words tumbled through him so fast he couldn't make sense of them.

"I can't hear you," he said, and the sound of his voice

pulled him up and out of his thoughts, racing him back to the present. He rocked on his hooves, off balance. The glowing spirits of Lightfeather, Morningleaf, and Grass-wing reared together and spread their wings. "Wait," Star cried, and then they cantered into the sky and flew up to the stars.

"What are you seeing?" asked Silverlake.

Star blinked, suddenly aware of the sounds around him: the sobbing, the terrified nickering, the confused bird singing, and the shuffling of hooves. Only a second had passed, and everyone was staring at him. He looked down and saw Morningleaf's crippled body quiver in the grass; and then it stiffened, took a final breath, and relaxed into empty stillness.

"Morningleaf is dead," he said with words as heavy as boulders, and yet inside he felt hollow, like the dry husk of an insect. Wails of grief rose from Sun Herd, and he could almost see the hope floating out of them, following Morningleaf to the golden meadow. Star felt the Sun Herd steeds give up.

He spread his wings over his best friend and let his tears wash her broken body. He was stunned by the depth of his sadness, which seemed to encompass the whole world, not just his best friend. The onlookers backed away, and even Silverlake moved so he could say good-bye alone.

After a long while Star stood and tucked his wings. His tears had created a wreath of white flowers around Morningleaf's body. Above him, the Hundred Year Star flared a final time—it was midnight.

24

FOLLOW ME

ALL OVER THE CANYON MEADOW, THE GATHERED pegasi arched their necks toward the sky. The Hundred Year Star swelled larger than the sun, but radiated no heat. Wings rose to shield sensitive eyes as the pegasi peeked through their feathers.

Star's heart thumped in his chest in a steady, hard wallop, like it was dying and then reviving with every beat. He faced his destiny, the Hundred Year Star, without flinching.

A gold ray of starlight unfolded from the round, fiery ball and dropped toward him like a tail. The closest steeds backed away, leaving him in an empty circle. Star folded his wings, waiting.

Silverlake, Echofrost, Bumblewind, Dawnfir, and Hazelwind inched as close to Star as they dared. A pegasus in the crowd whinnied, "Do something! Don't let the black foal receive his power."

Rockwing descended from his rock plateau. Cold fury lit his eyes, and they were trained on Star. "Look what you did, Destroyer," he said, pointing at Morningleaf. "You made Thunderwing kill his own filly."

Rockwing flared his wings and arched his neck for battle, his hooves dancing with energy. His intent was clear; he was going to kill Star himself.

"Enough!" neighed Thunderwing, and he dived off the rocks and barreled into Rockwing, spinning him across the grass. The two stallions reared and struck each other with their sharpened hooves. Both were deadly accurate, and soon blood was dripping steadily from their wounds.

The herds stampeded, and hundreds of pegasi fled the valley. Others snapped at enemy steeds, and fights broke out all over Canyon Meadow. Hazelwind galloped to help his sire, and Frostfire joined Rockwing. The four stallions battled while Star stood, silent and not moving. Twistfire soared into the melee, helping Rockwing, and Icewing came to Thunderwing's aid.

Star was all but forgotten as old enemies took the

opportunity to settle old scores, battling for power to the last incredible minute.

A brown colt with orange wings trotted from the other side of the pedestal rock. It was Brackentail. Like Star, he had grown.

Brackentail observed the chaos all around them and then his eyes settled on Morningleaf's body. "You killed her," he said flatly. "I always knew you would."

Star was so stunned he couldn't answer. With blinding clarity, he realized that Brackentail cared for Morningleaf. That was why he bullied Star and tried to keep Morningleaf away from him. He was jealous.

Star lowered his head, thinking. If Brackentail had killed him in the canyon run, Morningleaf would be alive right now. Star studied the colt's enraged expression and realized that it was grief. Brackentail returned his stare and then charged, seizing Star's neck with his teeth and ripping out a chunk of mane. Brackentail spit out the hair and struck with his hooves. Star dodged the blows, but he had no desire to strike back. Brackentail rammed into his chest, shoving Star backward. Star pushed the colt off him.

"I hate you," Brackentail said, spitting froth, and then resumed his attack, pummeling Star with kicks and hurled insults.

The tail of light from the Hundred Year Star crackled, and Star looked up. Brackentail paused in his assault, and the two colts stared at the incredible sparkling rays.

Silverlake whinnied.

Star glanced at her, and for the first time he saw her true age. She was deflated and looking as empty as he felt, but her eyes were determined. *"We're seeing this through, Star,"* she had said.

Rockwing broke free of Thunderwing and lunged at Star, followed by Brackentail. Jetfire and Oakfire landed near Star and protected him, blocking his attackers.

Star took a deep breath and kicked off the ground, flying toward the light. All across the valley the fighting faded, quelled by the sight of Star and his black shadow rising.

Star raced toward the golden light—his heart silent, his mind empty. He crashed into the golden beam in an explosion that paralyzed him. His body and wings went slack, but the light held him aloft. The power of it warmed him to his bones, vibrated every hair and feather on his hide, lighted the world, and blinded him at the same time. Star heard sizzling sounds, but he didn't feel anything except weightlessness.

An urge to yawn overwhelmed him. He opened his

mouth, and the starlight shot into him, forcing his jaws wider. The hot current invaded him, rattling his teeth, and flowed to the end of his tail and down through his hooves. His old and new wounds swelled and throbbed, but the pain oozed out of his body. His scabs melted, and fresh, healthy hair grew over them. He stretched his injured flank and noticed that it had been restored to perfection.

The starfire coursed through him, cleaning him, repairing him, and giving him strength. He tumbled in the sky like a creature caught in the ocean's waves, mouth open, until the last of the starlight had entered his body, and then everything went dark. Star free-fell back to land, head over tail. The steeds below scattered. He opened his wings at the last moment and landed gently on his hooves.

The steeds of Anok froze in place, tensed to bolt. Star scanned the herd, and wherever his eyes landed, pegasi cringed. His hide crackled with electricity. The hum of his power filled the valley, and he was warm with it, but otherwise he felt no different. The pegasi of Anok waited expectantly for him to do something, but he was rooted to the spot.

Thunderwing trotted cautiously to the black foal and kneeled before him. His body quivering as he spoke, "I submit myself to you for execution," he said to Star. "I've failed to perform my duties as over-stallion of Sun Herd." Thunderwing's voice was as cold and brittle as ice. He opened his crimson-red wings and closed his eyes, waiting for Star's deathblow.

A hush fell over the waiting steeds in the great meadow, and Star blinked at Thunderwing in disbelief.

"Seek your revenge, black foal," Thunderwing said, his expression anguished. "Please."

Star looked at the body of Morningleaf. Silverlake had arranged her into a more natural position, so she looked asleep. The white flowers surrounding her reminded him of the others who had passed—Lightfeather and Grasswing, all three sacrificed for this moment—and he didn't know what to do.

Star closed his eyes, and his mother's words came to him. "You know what to do," Lightfeather said. "I told you on the day you were born. Think. Remember."

The memories were unlocked; Star just had to find them. He chased the secrets, but they ran from him. He took a breath, relaxed, and finally her words slowly began to tickle his ears, the whispering growing louder until he could hear her clearly.

Many, many secrets poured forth, but one stood out.

One secret echoed Morningleaf's warning to him moons ago, thus doubling its impact on him. Lightfeather had repeated it more than once, and now he heard it again; he even thought he smelled his mother's warm, grassy breath. "Don't fight them. Heal them."

Star's eyes blinked open in shock. The pegasi of Anok watched him from the field, waiting, but he no longer saw an angry mob—he saw a bunch of terrified foals fighting all the wrong battles for all the wrong reasons.

Star folded his wings, and Lightfeather's gentleness washed over him. Morningleaf had been right all along— he would never win by fighting the pegasi on their terms, because their terms were always the same: to conquer one another. He had to change the rules, flip their thinking upside down, and his mother had told him how to do it.

He tapped Thunderwing on the shoulder. "Stand," he said.

The paranoid stallion eyed Star warily, but he stood.

"Breathe fire on them," Lightfeather said.

Star knew that when Nightwing breathed fire, he killed and destroyed, but his mother had said, "Trust the power of the star. You are good."

Star looked Thunderwing in the eyes, saw his guilt, and decided he had nothing to lose. "I will speak for

Morningleaf," Star said, and then he opened his jaws and roared golden starlight. It exploded out of him like an erupting volcano and engulfed Thunderwing. The stallion tried to run, but the light lifted him up in the air.

The pegasi of the five herds held still and watched in fear and awe.

"Star!" cried Silverlake. "What are you doing?"

Thunderwing galloped in place as the light enveloped him in heatless fire. Soon he gave up and dangled above the field with wings down. Star blasted him until the fear and guilt was burned out of Thunderwing's eyes. Star landed the stallion, closed his jaws, and the light vanished.

Thunderwing flexed his wings, blinking in astonishment. He was unharmed. He was better than unharmed. His battle wounds were healed, and all his pain, even the wounds of his heart, had been expunged. He glowed like a young colt.

"You are healed," Star said.

Tears pooled in the great stallion's eyes. He was speechless, shaken to his core—the anger that had shaped his posture and puffed his chest his entire life melted out of him like snow. He bowed to Star. "I submit my life to you, black foal."

Thunderwing's submission to Star drifted like a gentle

feather over the hushed steeds of Anok, floating on the collective air of their hot breath.

As they absorbed his words, some responded with confusion. "But they didn't fight," a mare whinnied.

Thunderwing trotted to Silverlake, and they leaned on each other over the body of their dead filly.

Oakfire sidled up next to Star, excited and nervous. "Shoot that fire on Rockwing," he said. "Make him bow to you."

Star glanced at Rockwing, whose expression was black with hatred, and shook his head. "He has to want it."

Oakfire swished his tail, fear and disappointment lighting his eyes. "So what good is this power then if you can't make them obey you?"

Star swept his wing over the thousands of pegasi gathered in the valleys—some were on their knees in awe, others were braced for war, and others were flexed for flight. "I'm not here to conquer them, Oakfire. Don't you think we've had enough of that?"

Oakfire looked perplexed.

Star had one more message to send to the five herds of Anok—a message they would not forget until the end of time, if it worked. Star's gut flipped with apprehension and hope. "Heal them," his mother had said, and maybe he could do one better than that.

Only the moon lit the valley now. Star walked to Morningleaf. He felt every eye on him, and he couldn't stop the trembling of his wings. If this didn't work, he would look foolish, and his heart would never mend. But when he looked at his broken friend, he knew only one thing for certain: she was worth the effort.

"Rise, Morningleaf," he said. He called on the seed of fire in his gut and drew it up into his throat. Sparks popped between his teeth and fell onto the grass. He opened his mouth and poured starfire over her, engulfing her fractured body.

Silverlake surged forward, squealing with fright, and Thunderwing held her back. The fire licked Morningleaf's feathers, ruffled her mane, and fluffed her tail. Behind her closed lids, Morningleaf's eyes glowed yellow.

Star swung his head, drenching her entire body in golden light until he was blinded by it.

Morningleaf floated off the ground. Her eyes opened. Her legs unfolded, and she stood on her own.

"It's impossible," Hazelwind whispered.

Star closed his mouth, and the light was extinguished. Standing before the five herds of Anok, on a bed of white flowers, was Morningleaf. Alive! She blinked a few times, adjusting to the scene around her. "What happened?" she asked, fluttering her aqua feathers.

Star whinnied, and Silverlake rushed to her filly, touching her and sniffing her. "It's my Morningleaf!" she said.

All over the vast meadow, hundreds more pegasi dropped to their knees, submitting to Star. The rest grumbled in varying states of anger, confusion, shock, or fear. "He's the healer," someone said.

"No!" trumpeted Rockwing. "If he can bring us back from the dead, then he has the power to destroy us too. He's more powerful than Nightwing."

His words caused a fresh stampede. Star looked at the pegasi of Anok with pity. He could force them to submit. He could make himself over-stallion of the five herds. He could be Starwing the Destroyer. A lot of the pegasi were ready for that and would willingly submit to him—they were already on their knees.

But the others, like Rockwing, were digging in their hooves in defiance—ready to battle him with their very souls. And some, like Twistfire, were addicted to war—their desire for control outweighing their need for peace. "Heal them" was Lightfeather's secret. "And forgive them," she'd commanded. He could do that, he thought. And he could start a new herd, one without an army or an over-stallion, one in which decisions were made in a group.

Star raised his voice and spoke to all who were gathered. "You don't have to fight me, or one another, anymore. Peace is your choice." He let his words carry through the valleys. "I am not the destroyer, but I cannot say the same for you." Star stared down the four remaining over-stallions, Frostfire, Twistfire, and all the steeds who stood with wings flared and jaws clenched. "I welcome all steeds who want to join me, but I won't be your over-stallion. I won't lead you, and I won't conquer you. Your lives are in your wings."

Star paused, catching the eye of Morningleaf, who nodded her head, encouraging him. Star exhaled, feeling unburdened for the first time since he was born. "Whoever would like to come may follow me." Star turned his back on the five herds of Anok and walked out of the valley like a common horse.

Morningleaf galloped to his side. "I'm with you," she said, her words lifting his heart.

"Wait for us, Star," said Bumblewind. Bumblewind and Echofrost followed, and then Silverlake and Thunderwing.

Hundreds more trotted behind them, following Star

out of the canyons.

When they were clear of the valley and crossing the mountain pass toward the Vein, Star looked back. Rockwing, Sandwing, and Smokewing were dividing up the remaining Sun Herd pegasi and forcing them to join their herds. Brackentail stood on the rock plateau with his eyes on Morningleaf, his expression ragged.

Five hundred pegasi trailed behind Star. To his surprise, one of them was Snow Herd's over-stallion, Icewing, Star's grandsire. The old silver pegasus wore an expression Star had never seen before on an over-stallion: hopefulness.

Star kicked off and led his herd into the sky. What the future held for them he didn't know, but he guessed that, one way or another, things would never be the same for the pegasi of Anok.

ACKNOWLEDGMENTS

THE FIRST PEOPLE I'D LIKE TO APPRECIATE FOR making this book possible are also the youngest people. From my agent's son, Zach, who gave *Starfire* a thumbs-up from the slush pile; to my daughter, who challenged me to write scenes that made her cry; to you, the reader! This story belongs to the children who care about it.

And now for the adults!

I'm forever thankful to my agent, Jacqueline Flynn, who read my manuscript and understood Star immediately. Describing him as a cross between Luke Skywalker and Rudolph the Red-Nosed Reindeer, Jacquie remains Star's passionate first advocate (and mine too!).

I'm grateful to editorial director Rosemary Brosnan

at HarperCollins Children's Books, who acquired *Starfire* and then infused the series with her enthusiasm and vision! It's an honor to work with Rosemary and her talented team of book lovers.

It's been equally thrilling to partner with Karen Chaplin, *Starfire*'s primary editor. Her suggested edits trimmed away all the unnecessary scenes and revealed the beating heart of the story beneath. She helped me bridle my wild manuscript and turn it into a well-behaved book, and for that I am grateful! I call her "the book whisperer."

A special thank-you goes to the artist who created the cover, the map, and the interior sketches—David McClellan. David captured the soul of *Starfire* in one epic book cover! (It took me an entire novel to convey the same thing, but I'm not jealous. Not at all.)

I'm also grateful for the outpouring of support from HarperCollins Children's Books, including: Marketing: Kimberly VandeWater. Publicity: Olivia DeLeon. Jacket and interior design: Sarah Nichole Kaufman. Sales: Andrea Pappenheimer and the whole sales team. And Library Outreach: Patti Rosati, Molly Match, and Preeti Chhibber. I can't thank you enough for giving the Guardian Herd book series the wings it needed to fly.

Personally, I'd like to thank my friends, church, and community for supporting my writing dreams long before this book was written—especially: Karen Perez, Mary Fletcher, Tracy Goodman, Angie Moberly, Julie and Traci Takasugi, Yvette Chester, Kathi Dalton, Bonnie and Salina Shelton, Kat Braunstein, Jennifer and Eva and Jay Ratcliffe, Jeannie Acuna, Rebekah Rocha, Jennifer Berndt, Shannyn Vehmeyer, Pat Hodgkin, Mariah Mullins, Desiree Rodriguez, Tamah Hulett, Jennifer Anderson, Shaylene King, and Angela Turpin.

And to everyone who knows me—thank you for understanding when I plunged into the land of Anok and disappeared for a while. I wish I could bring back souvenirs from my travels, but this book is all I have to offer. Maybe someday, somehow, I can take you with me.

I owe a special debt of gratitude to my favorite librarian on earth (next to my mother!). Gail Bland showed me that being an author is a state of mind, not a state of publication.

I'm blessed to have a fantastic family!

My husband thought I was crazy to try any career *besides* writing, but it took me awhile to believe that for myself. Thank you, Ramon, for encouraging me, believing in me, and dreaming for me. When I came to my senses, you made it easy for me—giving me the space and time I needed to write. I love you.

My family has cheered me on the whole way: my three kids—Nick, Crystal, and David; my parents—Charles and Sheila; my stepdad—Jeff; and my siblings—Daniel and Yuri, Angela and Jerry, Christian and Sarah, and Joel. You are in the book because you are in my heart.

Thanks to every horse I ever rode, even the ones that bucked me off!

Special love goes to Comet, the opinionated and loyal chestnut pony that is the inspiration for Morningleaf, and to my protective, motherly mare, Maddie, the inspiration behind Silvercloud.

Finally, I must give a special shout-out to my daughter. She woke up each morning while I was writing *Starfire* and read my chapters, never hesitating to tell me what I did wrong and what I did right. Her passion for the Guardian Herd series helped shape it into what it is today. I am forever grateful for the input, but more important, for the partnership. Someday, my dear filly, you will grow into those powerful wings, and I can't wait to see how far and how high you fly.

THE
⮜ GUARDIAN HERD ⮞

"Grasswing's Story"

By Jennifer Lynn Alvarez

Long before he was called Grasswing, honorary over-stallion of the Sun Herd walkers, the palomino pegasus was Grassfire, lead captain in Thunderwing's army. This is his story.

It was a spring day, forty-two seasons before the Hundred Year Star would appear in the sky, and Grassfire touched down in Dawn Meadow, having just returned from patrolling Sun Herd's borders. He'd spotted a large herd of land horses in the eastern Vein, the neutral land between his territory and Mountain Herd's, and he was excited to tell his colt, Graythorn, about them. The horses were lean, mostly brown in color, and they trotted together through the borderlands, seeking fresh grass and eating bark off the trees. As Grassfire galloped across Dawn Meadow, his hooves scattering spring flower petals and his long, flaxen mane teasing the wind, he wondered what it was like to be unable to fly, to touch only land and never clouds.

The midday sun blazed above, curling the grass with its heat, and the Sun Herd pegasi dozed in the shade, their wings fanning their backs. The foaling season, which often brought predators, had come and gone, and for the sixth season in a row, no foal was lost. This was no coincidence in Grassfire's mind, as it was also his sixth season as lead captain of the Sun Herd army.

After galloping for a few miles, Grassfire came closer to his herd and then slid to a halt, folding his pale-green wings and looking for Graythorn.

Mares and under-stallions abandoned the shade to greet him, trotting or flying across the meadow and collecting around him. Grassfire blew softly from his muzzle and greeted each steed. Thunderwing, the over-stallion of Sun Herd, didn't understand why he did this. But Thunderwing remained aloof from his herd, always at attention, socializing only with captains and his lead mare, Silvercloud. Grassfire enjoyed the company of all pegasi, from the youngest to the eldest.

"Where are the foals?" he asked Mossberry. "I want to tell them about the land horses I saw on my flight this morning."

The vibrant light bay mare flicked her tail and kicked off, whinnying, "Follow me."

Grassfire spread his large wings and rose up into the sky, flying after her. They coasted several miles across the grasslands until they reached Feather Lake, where the nursing mares and foals played and swam. When Grassfire glided over the dark-blue water, the foals burst into happy whinnying.

"Papa!" bleated Graythorn. The young colt swam across the lake, kicking his short legs as fast as he could. He was an exact replica of his sire, from his creamy mane and tail, to his pale-green feathers, to his full blaze, down to his one white sock. Their difference was in their size and color—where Grassfire's hide was golden, his son's was dark silver. "See how fast I can swim?"

"I do," said Grassfire, and his heart spilled over with affection for his colt. "Gather your friends, and I'll tell you all what I saw on my flight today."

"All right!" Graythorn swam to shore, bleating for the other foals.

Grassfire glanced around for his mate, Brightflower, and found her watching from the shoreline. She waved her wing at him, and he waved back. Brightflower was still battling the cough she'd acquired over the winter, and each spring she suffered persistent fevers. The medicine mare, Sweetroot, didn't know why Brightflower was plagued by so many illnesses, but they'd started when she was a filly. No one had expected her to live to adulthood, but she had, and Grassfire admired her quiet strength.

When Graythorn and his friends were settled on the sandy shore, gathered at Grassfire's hooves with their ears pricked forward and their eyes open wide, he began. "During my flight this morning, I saw an incredible sight." Grassfire squinted across the lake, pointing east with his wing. "In the Vein, between our territory and Mountain Herd's territory, I spotted a herd of land horses grazing, about a hundred of them."

The foals bleated with excitement. "A hundred horses! Can we see them?" asked Graythorn.

Grassfire shook his head. "No, son, they're too far away."

"Is it true they can't fly?" asked a bay filly.

"It is true," said Grassfire.

The filly spread her glossy feathers. "So they're like our walkers? Winged, but grounded?"

"Not quite," said Grassfire, amused. He knew these foals had never seen a land horse. "They have no wings at all."

The foals burst into horrified whispers. "That's terrible!"

"Which do you think is worse?" asked Grassfire. "To have wings but not be able to fly, or to have no wings at all?" He loved to rile the foals with difficult questions.

"Oh, it's worse to have no wings at all," answered the bay filly; and the other foals, including Graythorn, murmured their agreement.

Grassfire was about to ask the foals another question, but he was interrupted when a crimson feather landed on his muzzle. He looked up and saw Thunderwing blasting through the clouds, a wild look in his eyes. "Desert Herd raiders!" the over-stallion blared.

The mares leaped off the grass, instantly forming a tight circle around the foals. With ears pinned and tails lashing, they charged back to Dawn Meadow. Graythorn rallied his young friends with a battle cry, and Bright-flower trailed behind, wheezing hard. Mossberry flew to her side, encouraging her.

Grassfire met Thunderwing in the sky. "Where? How many raiders?"

"South, and I don't know—a lot, I hear. Silvercloud sent her scout back to warn us, but she stayed to count them. She'll return soon."

The two banked and soared back to Dawn Meadow, and Thunderwing trumpeted for the Sun Herd army.

Three thousand warriors lifted off and coasted over the forest of oaks that bordered the southern end of their expansive grassland.

As they approached, a light-gray figure shot through the trees; it was the lead mare, Silvercloud. Grassfire noticed her heavy breaths and rounded eyes. She was young for a lead mare, only fifteen, and this was her first experience with foreign invaders. "Two thousand stallions," she reported. "Coming from the coast."

"What?" Grassfire's feathers rattled. "That's not a raiding party; that's the entire Desert Herd army." The spring winds buffeted his mane, flipping it into his eyes.

"Are they in battle formation?" Thunderwing asked Silvercloud.

"They're on the ground, but they're in our territory."

"Are they hiding from us?"

"No, they are in the open," said Silvercloud.

Thunderwing lashed his tail, thinking. "All right, we'll intercept them. I'll leave a warrior squad here to protect the herd from predators." He nodded to Jetfire, the young, turquoise-winged stallion who rarely spoke but who always executed orders with flawless precision. "Jetfire, you'll command the predator squad; Silvercloud, you'll command the herd."

Jetfire and Silvercloud dipped their heads in quick agreement.

Grassfire took charge of his eight captains and their battalions. "Formation," he neighed, and they snapped to attention, gathering in angled rows sixty steeds wide and fifty steeds deep.

Thunderwing glanced at Silvercloud. "Keep the herd together and on the ground."

Her soft black eyes implored Thunderwing to stay safe, but she just nodded and whirled on the wind, soaring back to the meadow to command the herd.

Thunderwing addressed his army. "No stealth. We'll hit the Desert Herd steeds fast and hard, and drive them out."

Grassfire nodded. "Ready," he neighed.

Thunderwing trumpeted the call to battle, and his voice lifted on the winds and rumbled across the sky.

The Sun Herd army rocketed forward, ears pinned and jaws clenched. Grassfire took the lead, his muscles on fire as his warrior blood surged through his veins, and Thunderwing flew above them all, directing them and scanning the horizon as they soared toward their enemy.

"There," rasped Thunderwing an hour later, nodding toward a small, sparkling lake at the southern edge of their territory. It was located almost in the Vein—but not quite.

Grassfire looked and saw two thousand Desert Herd warriors standing at attention on the shoreline, watching the Sun Herd army approach. Instantly, he understood what they wanted. "They're thirsty."

"Hold," Thunderwing neighed to his army, and the three thousand warriors hovered in place with their wings whipping up the air currents. Grassfire flew to Thunderwing's higher altitude to consult with him. The over-stallion lashed his tail. "That's our water."

"True," said Grassfire, but he knew that east of the coast, Anok was in the midst of a three-year drought. Lack of rain and snowmelt had all but dried up Black Lake, which fed into the Tail River, Desert Herd's only source of drinking water besides the underground rivers, which were dangerous to approach. But the coastal fog and rain kept the Sun Herd lands green and the lakes full. "They're not here to fight," he said to Thunderwing.

"But they've crossed the Vein and our border. That's an act of war, especially when the intruders are all stallions. They must know that."

Grassfire nodded. And he couldn't deny that the sight of two thousand warrior enemies on Sun Herd's land excited his desire to fight, but he didn't think Desert Herd was here for that. The foreign warriors had folded their wings and lowered their heads. A moment later, a lone palomino with dark-yellow feathers lifted off and flew toward them. "Look, one of them is coming to speak to us," said Grassfire.

He recognized the palomino as Sandwing, the over-stallion of Desert Herd. He was tall and thin, his hide glossy like a flat lake in the morning. His deep chest curved into a waist so small Grassfire imagined his belly touched his spine. His wings were long and not very wide, but Grassfire knew Sandwing could fly higher and faster than any steed in Sun Herd and that a kick from his desert-hard hooves could topple a full-grown tree. The Desert Herd army was the most organized and ruthless in Anok, and yet their over-stallion approached the three thousand Sun Herd warriors alone. Grassfire knew without a doubt that Sandwing wasn't looking for a fight. He was desperate.

Thunderwing and Grassfire met the foreign stallion just below the coolness of the cloud layer. The tension was thicker than the wind, and Grassfire glanced at the Sun

Herd army, making eye contact with each captain. They understood. They were ready to attack if either over-stallion lost control.

Thunderwing would not disgrace himself by speaking first. He waited as Sandwing struggled to form words. "Thunderwing—" Sandwing began. Then silence again. Moments ticked by, and Grassfire saw how it pained the over-stallion of Desert Herd to ask for help. Finally, Sandwing croaked out his request. "My herd needs water."

Thunderwing stared at him, his eyes colder than death. "That is not my concern."

Sandwing pinned his ears, an act of aggression, and Thunderwing inhaled, ready to strike. Grassfire and his captains lunged forward just as Sandwing quickly lowered his gaze and flipped his ears forward.

"Stay back," Grassfire ordered his captains. He saw that Sandwing was struggling to remain submissive, but if his captains threatened the over-stallion too much, they might push him to violence, and then battle would be unavoidable.

Sandwing tried again. "I'm requesting your permission to water my mares, foals, and elders. My warriors won't drink, but . . . please . . . let the others."

Thunderwing gazed past Sandwing. "If your warriors

won't drink, then why are they here? And where are the others you speak of?"

"The others are resting on the beach by the ocean. The warriors are here . . ." He trailed off.

"Ah, in case I refuse," finished Thunderwing, flying forward so his muzzle was mere inches from Sandwing's. "Tell me, do you plan to fight for the water if I don't offer it?"

Fury roiled in Sandwing's eyes, but he breathed deep, forcing his muscles to stay relaxed. "The warriors are here to protect the herd from predators. That's all."

"So you won't fight for the water?" Thunderwing looked disappointed and irritated. He turned as if to fly away, as if bored with Sandwing.

Sandwing flashed his teeth. "I won't fight for the water . . . today."

Thunderwing whirled around, his eyes gleaming. The two finally understood each other. Sandwing would ask for the water today, or fight for it tomorrow, and he was letting Thunderwing decide which. "I'll discuss this with my captains," said Thunderwing. "Wait for my answer on the ground."

Sandwing rattled his feathers but obeyed, and Grassfire knew it crushed the over-stallion's soul to do so.

When Sandwing landed, Thunderwing faced Grassfire. "Call your captains."

Grassfire neighed for them and they flew to his side, leaving their battalions hovering over the scrubby grassland. When all had gathered, Thunderwing requested their advice. Three captains advised immediate attack. "They're weak. We can destroy Desert Herd today, gain access to their lands."

"Let the drought kill them," two other captains said.

"What about you?" Thunderwing asked, turning to Grassfire. "What do you think?"

The stallions quieted, watching Grassfire. He was older than Thunderwing and had never lost a battle. Each captain knew Grassfire could challenge Thunderwing for his position as over-stallion of Sun Herd and easily win, but Grassfire didn't want that—and it was because of decisions like this. If they refused Desert Herd the water, the steeds would grow weaker, and Sandwing would be forced to attack Sun Herd as a final resort; but it would be a slaughter. Looking down at Sandwing's warriors standing in the hot spring sun, Grassfire noticed they weren't sweating. They were already dangerously dehydrated. A battle with them would not bring pride or glory to Sun Herd. If Thunderwing let Desert Herd drink, an embarrassing slaughter could be avoided. Grassfire sighed. "I believe in fair fights."

Thunderwing nodded, understanding. "I agree, Grassfire. I'll let them drink here this summer, all of them. You tell Sandwing my decision."

Grassfire nodded, curved his wings, and dived toward the lake, landing on the shore. Up close, he saw that the Desert Herd warriors were in worse shape than he thought. Their eyes were dull and sunken, but their weak condition didn't prevent them from flaring their nostrils and rattling their feathers at him. Most were palominos, gold duns, and buckskins, and Grassfire's coloring fit right in with theirs; but his body did not. His frame was round with muscle and thick with bone, while these warriors were thin and light-bodied, reminding him of wasps.

Sandwing trotted forward, his eyes blazing with a dangerous mixture of fear, anger, and hopelessness. Grassfire reassured him. "You may drink from this lake for one summer."

Relief flickered across Sandwing's expression.

"All of you," he added, nodding toward the warriors.

Sandwing glanced up at Thunderwing hovering near the clouds and nodded. They would fight another time perhaps, but not today. Sandwing's eyes softened, but the words to thank Grassfire could not—would not—leave his mouth, and Grassfire didn't expect them; nor did he wait for them. He lifted off and rejoined Thunderwing.

The Sun Herd army flew back to Dawn Meadow in loose formation, feeling energized as their tension evaporated. They glided over the large herd of land horses that Grassfire had seen earlier, when he'd flown his morning border patrol. The horses were heading east, and Grassfire's captains brayed at them, making the horses spook into a gallop. "Poor beasts," said a captain. "Look at them; stuck on the ground, scared of their own shadows."

Grassfire's eyes darted to the land horses. They couldn't speak or think like pegasi, and he agreed that their bodies looked odd without wings, but Grassfire respected their grace on land. They leaped over boulders and fallen branches with ease, unlike the pegasi, who rarely jumped but who flew over obstacles instead. The horses had proud arched necks and agile hooves. "I don't feel sorry for them," he said, and the captains stopped their nickering.

The Sun Herd army flew the rest of the way home in silence, but when they swooped into Dawn Meadow, Grassfire was shocked to see loose feathers flying in the wind and blood on the soil. Dozens of Sun Herd steeds lay on their sides, groaning. "Brightflower!" He gasped, but he didn't see her among the wounded. He scanned the sky and the terrain, trying to piece together what had happened. "This isn't the work of predators," he neighed to Thunderwing. "Too many are injured. A bear or a puma could never have caused such damage."

Thunderwing pinned his wings and led the army to the ground. "What happened here?" he whinnied to Silvercloud. "Who did this?"

"Rockwing!" she cried. "He raided us."

Grassfire blinked back his shock. Mountain Herd scouts must have been spying, and when they saw Sun Herd's army fly south, they seized the chance to attack. Grassfire scanned the injured steeds. He knew them all, but a large group was missing. "The foals," he whispered.

"Yes," whinnied Silvercloud. "Rockwing took them."

"All of them?" asked Thunderwing.

"No. My mares rushed a group into the woods."

Grassfire inhaled hard, his breath ripping at his lungs. "Where's Graythorn?"

Silvercloud wrung her wings. "He wouldn't leave Brightflower. She had a coughing fit, and she fell. She's okay. But Graythorn . . ."

Silvercloud glanced east, toward Mountain Herd's territory. "He was taken."

Fear shot through Grassfire's veins, turning his hot blood cold. Rockwing carried no honor among the over-stallions of Anok. He struck like a coward, when herds were weak, and for no respectable reason. Mountain Herd was healthy, their numbers growing each season, and Rockwing didn't need more foals. He took them merely to weaken Sun Herd. And now he had Graythorn.

Grassfire flew across Dawn Meadow to find Brightflower. There she was, panting in the shade. He landed and pressed his forehead against hers. "I'll get Graythorn back," he promised. She coughed, holding her sides with her wings, and he saw she was in terrible pain. "Is your chest hurting again?" he asked. Sometimes sharp pains racked her heart and made her cry.

"No, I'm just . . . Graythorn tried to protect me," she whispered, her breath hitching. "Even as they dragged him away. Tell our colt I'm proud of him."

Grassfire swept her forelock aside. "You can tell him yourself, after I rescue him."

Her eyes, swollen from crying, warmed. "All right,"

she said, and her voice was like the breeze, smelling of grass and wildflowers.

He blinked at her, overwhelmed. She was lying like a foal, curled in the grass. Her spotted hide was gleaming and her violet feathers sparkling in spite of her ill health, and her sweet beauty crushed him. His heart belonged to Brightflower—and Graythorn belonged to them—and the three of them did not belong apart. "I'll return to you soon," he said. "With Graythorn."

She nodded as fresh pain stole her breath.

Grassfire lifted off to join Thunderwing and Silvercloud, who hovered over the meadow assessing the damage to the herd.

"Where's Jetfire?" Thunderwing asked his mate.

"He followed the stolen foals," said Silvercloud.

"By himself?"

"Yes, so he wouldn't be seen."

Thunderwing nodded. "Good. Please see to the mothers."

Silvercloud landed to soothe the distressed mares, and Thunderwing neighed for the eight captains, calling them and Grassfire to meet on the ground beneath a giant weeping willow tree. When they were all present, a pinto captain spoke. "We should attack now. Immediately." His filly was one of the captured.

"Yes. Now!" whinnied another, whose filly had also been taken.

"No!" Grassfire saw how his captains' anguish changed them—from unflappable warriors to hotheaded stallions. "Rockwing wants this," he said, thinking aloud. "He'll expect a swift and thoughtless attack from Sun Herd. We must plan strategically."

"But our army is bigger," neighed the pinto captain. "What do we stand to lose?"

Grassfire flattened his ears. "We stand to lose the foals."

"They're already gone!" The pinto's gaze slashed across the meadow and locked on the distant border of Mountain Herd's territory.

"But they're still alive," said Grassfire.

The captain whinnied in Grassfire's face. "You don't know that!"

Grassfire whirled and slammed the pinto in the chest with his hind hooves, knocking him down. Then he faced the others, searching their faces for defiance but seeing none. The downed captain stood up, shook the grass off his back, and nodded to Grassfire. The swift kick had returned him to his senses.

Thunderwing exhaled. "Grassfire is right. We will attack, but let's think first."

Silvercloud's voice reached them from a distance. "There's Jetfire!" she neighed.

Grassfire watched as the cream-colored captain glided over the heads of the Sun Herd pegasi and landed beneath the weeping willow. His hide dripped sweat, and his sides heaved. "The foals are being held in Valley Field," he said, wasting no time. "Rockwing's warriors spotted me and gave me a message."

Grassfire tensed, searching for signs of injury to Jetfire, but he saw none.

Jetfire delivered the message. "If we cross the Vein into their territory, they'll kill the foals, all of them. If we don't, they'll keep the foals and raise them as their own."

Thunderwing threw back his head and trumpeted his rage.

"It's better that they die then live with Mountain Herd," spat the youngest captain.

"What sort of game is Rockwing playing?" Grassfire wondered aloud. Did he steal foals because his were born dead? He'd lost seven colts with his mate, Birchcloud, including one this season. Was he mad with grief? Grassfire couldn't guess, but he had a plan to save the stolen foals. "I think I can rescue the foals, but I'll need Desert Herd's help."

Thunderwing pricked his ears, listening.

"I'll take a small battalion from Sun Herd. We'll gallop into Valley Field, take our foals, and be back before Mountain Herd knows what happened," said Grassfire.

"How?" Thunderwing asked. "You'd have to go at night, and they'll expect that."

"No, that's where Desert Herd comes in. I'll do it in broad daylight."

Jetfire tossed his mane. "Sentries are posted all over the mountains, Grassfire. You'll never make it into Valley Field unseen, and if you do, the foals will be killed before you arrive. There is no way for you to sneak up on them. It's impossible."

Grassfire lifted his head. "It's not. Listen." The captains and Thunderwing gathered closer as Grassfire explained how his idea could work.

After he received approval from Thunderwing, Grassfire assembled an agile battalion of fifty warriors. Thunderwing prepared the larger army for what might come next. If Grassfire was successful and made off with the foals, Rockwing's army would likely follow them back to Sun Herd. Thunderwing, his warriors, and his battle mares would meet them at the border.

Grassfire kicked off and flew south, followed by his battalion. They glided over the oak forest and landed just as the sun set. They would shelter for the night, then approach Desert Herd in the morning. His plan was crazy, he knew it, but that's why he was sure it would work. As Grassfire appointed a night sentry and closed his eyes to rest, he hoped Sandwing would agree to help him.

The next morning Grassfire and his warriors rose with the sun and flew toward the lake where Thunderwing had given Sandwing permission to drink. They crested the oak forest, and below them was all of Desert Herd. Sandwing had called the nursing mares and elders up from the coast to drink, and when they spotted Grassfire, they neighed for Sandwing.

"Hold here," Grassfire said to his battalion. He descended in a slow circle, alone, and met Sandwing on the shore where they'd spoken earlier.

Sandwing pinned his ears, his expression suspicious. "What is this?" he asked, looking up at the battalion hovering overhead.

Grassfire quickly explained what had transpired at

Dawn Meadow and his idea to save the Sun Herd foals.

Sandwing exhaled, folding and refolding his wings. Then he asked, "Can we still drink at this lake all summer if I refuse your request?"

Grassfire balked. "Do you believe I lack honor? Of course you can."

Sandwing glanced at his herd, and Grassfire followed his gaze, noticing that his steeds were already much revived. Sandwing made up his mind. "We will help you take back your foals."

Relief surged through Grassfire, and Sandwing whistled for the highly trained mares who Grassfire had requested: the sky herders. Forty of them lifted off, coasted to their over-stallion, and landed. Sandwing explained to them their mission. They were going to drive the herd of land horses straight into Valley Field with Grassfire and his team hiding among them. The scent of the horses and the dust from the stampede would conceal the pegasi from the Mountain Herd scouts.

Grassfire watched the sky-herding mares as they listened to their leader. They were small with wiry muscles, and they moved as one—like a swarm of bees—but their eyes glittered with cunning intelligence. A golden buckskin mare twisted her long neck and stared at Grassfire, her eyes bulging as she received Sandwing's instructions. Then she introduced herself to Grassfire. "I'm Sunblaze, leader of the sky herders."

Grassfire dipped his head to her. "I'm Grassfire, lead captain of Sun Herd."

Her lip curled with distaste when he said "Sun Herd," but she quickly stuffed her feelings. "Are you ready?" she asked him.

Grassfire nodded, and the mares lifted straight up into the sky with a rapid whoosh of wingbeats. Grassfire trumpeted for his battalion, and everyone followed the mares. "I last saw the land horses heading east," he said.

Sunblaze flattened her ears. "We have our own scouts. We know where they are." She flew behind her mares and guided them with a complicated series of whistles and clicks.

Grassfire and his warriors drafted in the mares' wake, and he wished Sun Herd knew the ancient skills and language of the sky herders. Only Desert Herd and Mountain Herd possessed that knowledge, and they didn't share it. The skills were useful not just in battles, but also in raids, for confusing predators, and to gather foals quickly. Sky herders were small—always mares—agile and quick. Unlike warriors, they were taught to think on their own but also to work as a group. They trained for years and seemed to read one another's minds, but they were constantly communicating in their secret language. He'd seen them in action, years ago, herding a Sun Herd patrol into an ambush, and he still didn't understand how they did it—how they tricked their enemies into deadly traps.

Grassfire and the sky herders soon arrived at the base of the mountains bordering Valley Field. "There are the horses," said Sunblaze.

Up close, Grassfire saw that he'd been right. There were about a hundred of them. Their lead stallion spotted the flying pegasi and pricked his ears. He was black, a color that was not uncommon for horses but was unique for pegasi. Only the special pegasus foals born under the Hundred Year Star were black, and most of them died at birth.

Sunblaze coasted to Grassfire's side. "Join the horses. They'll be afraid of you, but stay with them. We'll make sure to herd you all into Valley Field."

"Thank you," said Grassfire, and Sunblaze's eyes widened at his words. She dipped her head and whistled commands to her mares.

Grassfire spoke to his warriors. "When we hit the ground, fold your wings around your chests. The dust from the stampeding land horses will disguise us, but if you spread your wings, you'll give us away to the Mountain Herd scouts. Watch the horses, imitate them, and keep up with the herd. They're fast on land, and they jump like deer. Don't underestimate them, and don't speak. It will spook them worse."

Grassfire led his team to the forest floor, where they landed softly beside the land horses. The black stallion reared, and his lead mare tore into the woods followed by the rest of the herd—all mares and foals. The stallion took the rear.

Grassfire and his warriors wrapped their wings around their chests and galloped into the midst of the horse herd. The horses' eyes rounded in terror, but Sunblaze and her mares charged around them, darting between the trees, whistling and clicking, and guiding the stampeding herd to the narrow mountain pass that led to Valley Field. Once they entered the pass, the horse herd wouldn't be able to turn around. The mares would peel off and return to the lake. Grassfire thundered through the forest, excitement powering his haunches.

The horses entered the pass as if it were their choice to go there, but clearly it wasn't. The black stallion was furious and confused. Over the centuries, the simple horses had learned the boundaries of the pegasi lands, and they stuck to living in the Vein because they were afraid of pegasi. When horses accidentally wandered into their territories, the pegasi drove them off—to preserve their grasslands from other grazing creatures. So Grassfire knew this stallion didn't want to gallop madly into Valley Field, but he had no choice. The desert mares were using the horses' herd instincts against them.

When Sunblaze saw that the horses had fallen for her plan and could not turn their stampede around, she called off her mares. They lowered their heads and walked back toward the lake, hiding their wings to look like horses from the sky.

Grassfire glanced upward and saw a Mountain Herd patrol flying overhead, but their bodies were relaxed, their expressions amused. It was working. They didn't see a threat, just a herd of frightened horses.

Grassfire, his fifty warriors, and the horse herd exploded out of the pass, startling a second group of Mountain Herd pegasi who were watching the foals. The guards lifted off over the foals' heads, gathered into attack formation, and then nickered to one another. "It's just horses," one neighed.

Grassfire took stock. There were thirty warriors

guarding the foals, and the Mountain Herd army was not in sight, but they were probably nearby. His team didn't have much time. Soon the Mountain Herd steeds would realize the stampede was a ruse. Grassfire and his battalion surrounded the foals, who immediately recognized their herdmates.

Graythorn galloped to Grassfire's side. "Papa, I knew you'd come for us."

Grassfire beamed at him. "Let's go home," he whinnied.

The Sun Herd warriors turned and bolted back toward the pass with the foals in tow. The Mountain Herd scouts stared in confusion. "The foals are running away with the horses!"

Grassfire snorted. His plan was working. Mountain Herd still didn't understand.

But suddenly a trumpeting cry reverberated through the pass—it was Rockwing. He was returning from the Vein and flying with a squadron of warriors. Grassfire's heart thudded. This was bad timing. He and his team were galloping straight toward Rockwing with the foals, and they would have to pass right under him.

Rockwing paused, hovering in the sky and staring at them, but his confusion was short-lived. "Those aren't horses!" he brayed.

Rockwing and his warriors dived like hawks, tackling the Sun Herd pegasi.

"Fly," Grassfire neighed to the foals. They were young and had not flown higher than the trees, but the winds were still today. They could do it if they tried. Suddenly, a hoof clubbed Grassfire in the back, and he had no more time to think. He reared, snatched his attacker, and hurled him into a tree. Two more dropped on him from above, and Grassfire entered the battle of his life.

The foals had lifted off, led by Graythorn, and Grassfire lost track of them. He fought steed after steed without a break, and without a chance to look around. Soon Rockwing's entire army would arrive; he was certain of it. He and his small team forced their way through the pass, one battle at a time, defeating Rockwing's patrol warriors. Hours seemed to pass, but it could have been only moments. Then, behind him, Grassfire suddenly heard the humming of thousands of wings—Rockwing's army was coming.

A voice wafted from above. "Papa, don't give up!"

Grassfire kicked the warrior who was attacking him and knocked him out. "Graythorn," he whinnied. "Where are you?"

"Up here."

Grassfire looked up and squinted. Graythorn was high above him, dangling in the grip of two Mountain Herd warriors. Anguish drained his blood. Graythorn's eyes glittered with fury as he tried to bite the warriors. "I found the sky herders," his colt neighed to him. "They've sent for Thunderwing. He's coming with the whole Sun Herd army!" Graythorn kicked at his attackers and blasted one in the shin. "Put me down!"

Grassfire couldn't breathe. His colt's life was in the jaws of his enemies. Brightflower's face flashed across his mind.

The over-stallion of Mountain Herd looked down at Grassfire. "You think you're smart," he said. "But I'm smarter."

Rockwing's army appeared behind him—two thousand five hundred steeds with sharpened hooves and bared teeth—and Grassfire was still in their territory, still in the mountain pass. But Graythorn had said Thunderwing was coming, and hope bloomed in Grassfire's heart.

Rockwing trumpeted the call to battle, and Grassfire lashed his tail. The entire Mountain Herd army descended into the pass.

"Papa!" screamed Graythorn.

Grassfire and his fifty warriors faced the army. They couldn't win this fight, but his son's words echoed in his mind: *Papa, don't give up!*

Grassfire pinned his ears. "Charge!" He led his warriors into Rockwing's front line.

"Look!" whinnied Graythorn.

Grassfire couldn't turn around, but he listened and he heard the battle cry of Thunderwing. Relief soaked his bones. Thunderwing's three thousand warriors dropped into the pass and clashed with Rockwing's army. Steeds battled all around; but Sun Herd's army was bigger, and they pressed hard on Rockwing's warriors, driving them back toward Valley Field.

Amid the sounds of breaking bones, grunts, and shrieks of fury, Grassfire heard his name and looked up. Rockwing hovered overhead, directing his warriors, but now his black eyes focused on Grassfire. "Your colt will pay for this, Grassfire." His warriors still had Graythorn's wings gripped in their teeth, and his colt was trying to kick loose but tiring fast.

Grassfire launched off the ground and hurtled toward Rockwing, but ten Mountain Herd warriors intercepted him. They snatched his wings and dragged him back toward land. Grassfire fought them, striking with his ice-sharp hooves and deadly teeth. Three stallions seized his right wing and another three stallions took his left.

Grassfire bucked, trying to throw them off, trying to fly to his captured colt, but the Mountain Herd steeds held him tight. The other four stallions kicked at him but couldn't get too close without getting struck themselves. Grassfire killed one and set his sights on the others, but the six stallions, three at each wing, began to pull in opposite directions. Pain flared, hot and brilliant, in his shoulders, and he clamped his jaws shut to keep from screaming.

"Papa!" sobbed Graythorn. "Somebody help him!"

Thunderwing heard the colt's call, and he whirled to see Grassfire's wings being stretched wide. Thunderwing brayed for help and charged Grassfire's attackers with twenty warriors of his own. The stallions holding Grassfire's wings yanked hard, and all shame left Grassfire as he bleated his pain like a newborn foal, unable to stop himself. He felt tendons and muscles ripping all along his shoulders and up into his wings, and Grassfire reeled, the forest turning black. The last thing he saw were his colt's wild eyes as Thunderwing drove off Grassfire's attackers, and then Grassfire melted into the dirt, unconscious.

Grassfire awoke in Dawn Meadow. "Shh, don't move," said the medicine mare, Sweetroot.

"Graythorn!" he cried, his words strangling his dry throat.

His mate, Brightflower, was near, and she nuzzled him. Grassfire looked at her and gasped. She seemed ancient. Her eyes were swollen and her ears drooped; her teeth chattered as if she were freezing, but the day was warm. He blinked rapidly, glancing around him. "What happened?"

Brightflower wept so hard she couldn't speak. Sweetroot, who he'd never seen cry, also burst into tears. Frustration churned his gut. "Tell me what happened?" He tried to stand, to fly, but fiery pain scorched his shoulders and shot through his body. He collapsed in the grass, and his muscles twitched.

Silvercloud landed next to him and pressed her soft feathers against his forehead. "Don't move, and I'll tell you what happened as I heard it."

He nodded, his head throbbing.

"When you sent the foals off, after Rockwing first showed up in the pass, Graythorn took the lead. On his way out he spotted the Desert Herd mares, and he begged them to take the message to Thunderwing that you were in trouble. They're fast flyers, faster than foals, and they agreed." She sighed. "A few mares helped the foals home, but Graythorn did not come back here with them. Instead he returned to you."

Grassfire closed his eyes. He knew Graythorn had saved him and his warriors, but why didn't his colt stay where he was safe?

As if reading his mind, Silvercloud said, "The mares didn't argue with Graythorn. They said they didn't want to tangle with the future over-stallion of Sun Herd."

Grassfire exhaled in a gasp because he knew it was true. Graythorn would grow to challenge Thunderwing when he was older. Everyone knew it, including Thunderwing, and apparently even strangers knew it. He nodded.

Silvercloud continued. "Sun Herd won the battle against Mountain Herd's army in the pass. Rockwing retreated and escaped, but Graythorn—he did not survive."

Grassfire groaned as the news slammed him like a hard kick. Now he understood why Brightflower looked ancient. Grassfire tried again to stand, shaking his head. "Where is he? How do you know he's dead? Maybe they decided to keep him?"

Silvercloud shook her head, her eyes filling with tears. "He's here. He's next to Brightflower."

Grassfire craned his neck, and there, next to his mate, stretched across the grass, was Graythorn. His eyes were closed; he was still and quiet, as if he were sleeping. His pale-green wings were broken. "His wings?" Grassfire rasped.

Silvercloud said it fast, sparing Grassfire a drawn-out explanation. "Rockwing broke his wings and dropped him from the clouds. He died quickly."

Grassfire bent in half as grief that was worse than any physical pain tore through every fiber of his body and soul. Graythorn was gone. His colt was dead.

Next to him Brightflower wept, and Grassfire buried his muzzle in hers. "I'm so sorry," he cried. "I didn't bring him back to you. I failed."

"No, no," she whispered, pressing her forehead against his. "Graythorn brought *you* back to *me*. I'm proud of my colt, and of you. All the foals are home. And Graythorn— he's right beside me. We can bury him here, in Dawn Meadow."

"There's something else you must know, Grassfire," said Sweetroot, wiping her eyes. She paused. "The injuries to your wings . . . they're permanent. You won't fly again. Not ever."

Grassfire stared at her, uncomprehending.

"I'm sorry," she said.

"That's impossible."

"I'm so very sorry," said Sweetroot, and Grassfire slipped back into unconsciousness.

Two long years passed before Grassfire accepted his disability, and six years after that, Brightflower's ill health finally claimed her and she died. It was ten more years before he accepted her death, and then the following year Thunderwing appointed him leader of the Sun Herd walkers and granted him the honorary title of Grasswing. From then on Grasswing accepted everything that came to him, good or bad, immediately.

The Sun Herd steeds noticed the change in him—his peacefulness—and soon they were flocking to him for advice on matters not just of war, but also of love, illness, loneliness, and everything in between. And Grassfire found new life as a mentor to the yearlings. It started simply enough, with colts and fillies gathering to hear his battle tales, but then they returned for advice on entering the Sun Herd army; and he helped them find their paths, answering their questions with questions of his own, making them think for themselves, and helping them decide what was most important to them.

Over time he came to think of each and every Sun

Herd foal as his own young Graythorn, and each seemed to embody something of his son. They were curious, or brave, or stubborn, or smart, or just plain silly—like Graythorn had been when he wasn't trying to take charge. They were full of hope and excitement for the future, and through them his heart was renewed, through them his sadness was buried. And Grasswing thrived as a walker. He couldn't fly, but he was grateful for each morning that the sun rose on his strong body, joyful that he could still gallop like the wind, and proud that he protected his fellow walkers as their honorary over-stallion.

But Grasswing never accepted the horrific death of Graythorn. Rockwing's act against his colt was too cruel to let pass. Instead, he waited for the day he could battle Rockwing one-on-one, with no armies, no hostages, and no wings—a battle on the ground and to the death. And Grasswing never imagined winning or losing this battle; he just longed for the chance to face Rockwing and to fight the fight that Graythorn had lost.

And when it was over, win or lose; he would look forward to his final destination: the golden meadow. Graythorn and Brightflower were there, and they would fly together—the three of them—migrating across Anok, their feathers brilliant streaks of green and violet light—reunited forever.

Turn the page for a sneak peek
at the second epic adventure in

THE
GUARDIAN
≈ HERD ≈
SERIES

1

INTRUDER

STAR KICKED OFF THE GRASS AND FLEW INTO THE
currents on the tail of Hazelwind, four stallions, and two
battle mares. The sky was clear, and Star found it difficult
to judge his altitude without the clouds. He was a good
flier now, but he was still getting used to his powerful
wings and to the confusing perspective of the heights. He
glanced upward, wanting to soar higher, but Hazelwind
leveled out when the air grew thin.

Star glanced at the fliers around him, noticing their
chests expanding and falling too fast, their bodies shivering, and their eyes leaking tears. This was high enough
for them, but the starfire he'd received a moon ago on his
first birthday filled his belly, pulsing through him and

warming him, and Star had no trouble breathing. He tamped down his longing to fly higher and focused instead on the mission.

"Eyes down," Hazelwind neighed over the ripping currents. Hazelwind's dam was Silverlake, the past lead mare of Sun Herd, and she'd asked her adult colt to patrol the skies. They circled above the Vein where their herd lived and grazed. Earlier, Hazelwind had spotted the hoofprints of an intruder, and he'd invited Star and some others to help him search for the stranger.

"You're sure we're not looking for a horse," whinnied Dewberry, a small but fierce battle mare. She was four years old and Star didn't know her well, but Hazelwind did. They'd met in Sun Herd's old army.

Hazelwind flicked his ears at her. "Horses don't travel alone."

"Neither do pegasi," she countered.

Hazelwind snorted, and his wing caught the edge of a wind current, sending his body into a spiraling roll. Dewberry nickered in delight as Hazelwind struggled to right himself. When he was gliding safely again, he explained. "A lone horse wouldn't come so close to us, Dewberry, but a spy would."

"A horse spy?" she asked, blinking her large eyes.

Hazelwind opened his mouth to answer, but Dewberry darted ahead, flicking her tail at him.

Star nickered, amused by the banter between the steeds and feeling joyful to be part of a herd and, more than that, to be flying. After Star received his power from the Hundred Year Star, he'd settled his followers in the Vein along the western coast of Anok, near Crabwing's Bay. He called them River Herd in honor of the deep, winding waterway that had led them from the heart of Mountain Herd's territory to the sea.

Five hundred steeds had followed Star out of Rockwing's Canyon Meadow and into an unknown future. Since then, two hundred more had abandoned their herds, risking execution from their over-stallions, to join Star. They had been surviving in the Vein for the last moon, but Star knew he had to find them a home, and quickly. The pregnant mares were nervous and impatient. Some longed to return to Sun Herd's lands, but Star chose not to claim his old territory. It was surrounded by herds that were hostile to him and to the steeds who'd joined him. War could not be avoided if they returned there.

And Star wanted a new beginning for River Herd, a territory unscathed by battle and the devastating memories of the past. But the decision was not his alone, for he was not the over-stallion of River Herd, and neither was Thunderwing. The mighty crimson-feathered bay had given up his power when he followed Star, and he was now known as Thundersky. Star had formed a council to govern River Herd. They met daily to discuss their future, and Star trusted that an appropriate home would be decided upon soon.

In the meantime, River Herd lived peacefully in the Vein, but trouble it seemed had found them.

Star and the others scanned the terrain far below their hooves. The great river that had led them to the coast was just a thin blue line, the trees were shapeless green clumps, and the grazing River Herd pegasi were the size of ants. Star squinted his eyes, and things became clearer. He could make out the colors of the pegasi, even spotting Morningleaf's aqua feathers. From there he surveyed the terrain, sectioning it into shapes so he wouldn't miss anything.

Suddenly a movement caught Star's eye, so stealthy he might have imagined it. He blinked, shaking his head.

"Did you see something?" asked Hazelwind.

"I thought so, but I can't be sure."

The patrol tensed, and Dewberry spoke. "Trust your eyes, Star."

He had seen movement, and she was right; he shouldn't doubt his own eyes. "Yes, I saw something."

"Take us to it," Hazelwind said, ears pinned.

Star curled his wings, held them tight, and plunged headfirst. The eight others followed, plummeting toward land like diving hawks. Star narrowed his eyes against the sharp wind, his teeth rattling and his wings shaking as he sliced through the crosscurrents, picking up speed. The curve of the horizon flattened as the ground raced toward him, ready to slam into him, but everything also became clearer, easier to see. The individual rocks, the leaves, and the thing that had trotted across his vision, its color blending so it was almost invisible. With another sudden movement, the figure appeared in sharp relief. "It's a puma," Star whinnied.

"I see it," said Hazelwind.

The big tawny cat was stalking a small palomino yearling who had drifted away from the herd to graze on fresh grass. Star whistled a warning to her.

"No!" Hazelwind neighed to Star, but it was too late.

Star's throat tightened as he watched the palomino react to his warning. She spread her wings to fly away but only made it several feet up in the air before the leaping puma's claws sank into her feathers. The cat dragged her to the ground, and within seconds it had its jaws around her throat.

Hazelwind hurtled past Star and rammed the big cat. The stallion, the palomino, and the puma tumbled across the grass. Star and the others landed, surrounding Hazelwind. Dewberry kicked the puma until it let go of the yearling, who then raced away on hoof, her injured wings fluttering behind her. The big cat backed toward the trees, hissing and spitting, then turned and ran.

Star was confused and shocked. "I'm sorry," he said. He would have to do better to protect his herd.

Hazelwind landed and folded his wings. "Movement attracts cats, Star. We had time to reach the yearling before the puma attacked her, but once she bolted, it had to act." Hazelwind took a deep breath. "But don't be upset. You spotted the creature, and that ultimately saved the palomino's life. You did well. Let's go see how she is."

Star and the patrol returned to River Herd. The medicine mare was already tending the palomino, packing her wounds with leaves. "Would you like my help?" Star asked her. He hadn't healed anyone since he'd brought Morningleaf back to life on his birthday.

Sweetroot shook her head. "The fangs just grazed her. She's sore and she lost some hair and feathers, but it's nothing my herbs can't cure."

The palomino yearling, a refugee from Desert Herd, was trembling. "We don't have cats where I live," she said, tossing her mane. "I mean . . . where I used to live."

Star remembered the night this filly arrived. She'd escaped with her family, but her parents and siblings had been caught and killed by Desert Herd warriors. She'd only survived because she'd gone to a river to drink and the patrol hadn't seen her. When she arrived in the Vein, she was almost dead with exhaustion and terror.

Star's wings sagged with sorrow. He looked at Sweet-root, who'd been treating his wounds and counseling him since the day he was born. "This is my fault. We need an army."

Sweetroot nickered. "Calm yourself, Star. Armies are for war."

"But the herd needs protection."

"Protection and war are two very different things."

"Are they?" Star drew up his wings and trotted away, more confused than ever. What sort of black foal was he if his herd wasn't safe even from cats? Thundersky would never have let a cat near his herd.

As Star walked, he felt the questioning eyes of the others on him, so he cantered into the sky where he could think.

He soared through the clouds, glancing down to see

Hazelwind's patrol meeting with River Herd's council of leaders to discuss the puma. Star worried that they hadn't spotted the hooved intruder since the attack. He or she was either hiding very well or had left. Star cruised just over the trees and was not surprised when his best friend, Morningleaf, appeared beside him. They flew together in silence, and after a while his breathing slowed and his thoughts calmed. Finally he broke the silence. "I don't know what I'm doing."

Morningleaf nickered. "Of course you don't; you're a yearling."

"But I'm the black foal. They expect me to know things, to save them. What was I thinking starting a new herd? We don't have a territory or an army. It's winter, and we should be flying south by now, but I don't know where to go."

Morningleaf angled her aqua feathers and banked right. Star followed her. "The council will find us a home, Star. Remember Mossberry's stories—about the ancient pegasi who lived in the interior, on the windy plains? If those lands truly exist, they're not in use. My mother told me we might move there."

Star remembered Mossberry's stories well. She was an elder mare who'd befriended him on his first migration. Neither she nor Star could fly so they migrated with the walkers, and Mossberry had entertained him with stories and legends about the pegasi. A violent forest fire had taken her life on that journey, and Star shuddered at the memory. He looked at Morningleaf. "I remember hearing about the interior of Anok, but we have pregnant mares. We can't waste time traveling to land that may not be habitable."

Morningleaf glanced at him. "Don't worry so much. Things will work out—for the best." Her amber eyes were soft, unconcerned. Her trust in him surpassed reason, but it calmed him too. She dropped and landed in a clearing surrounded by fir trees. Star touched down beside her. "Look at all this sweet, untouched grass," she said.

They lowered their heads and grazed, enjoying the winter sun on their feathers. Before long, rustling leaves drew Star's attention toward the woods. He pricked his ears as a shape creeped through the shadows. Slowly it walked toward them, and every muscle in Star's body tensed. Morningleaf reacted too, lifting her wings, poised for flight. They each froze, listening. Then the shadowy creature stepped into the light. Star's gut dropped, and Morningleaf sucked in her breath.

There, standing in front of them was Brackentail— the Betrayer. The orange-feathered colt said the last two words Star expected to hear. "Help me."

2

THE BETRAYER

STAR AND MORNINGLEAF STOOD ROOTED TO THE ground. They stared at the brown yearling colt who had helped Rockwing plan his battle against Sun Herd only a moon ago, a battle that resulted in many deaths, including Star's mentor, Grasswing. As Brackentail staggered closer, Star and Morningleaf each took a step back, training their eyes on him.

"Please, help me," Brackentail repeated, wheezing as though he had holes in his lungs.

Star scanned the yearling's body. Brackentail was thin and covered in dried blood. His eyes were swollen, almost shut; his tail was chewed to shreds; half his mane had been pulled out; and he had a broken wing.

The orange-feathered limb hung to the ground and had clearly been dragged over weeds and bushes for a long distance. The end feathers were torn, and the longest ones were missing, yanked out by their roots. The healthy wing rested on Brackentail's back. Flies infested his wounds and crawled over his face as though the colt were already dead. "What happened to you?" Star asked.

Brackentail lowered his head. "Rockwing banished me from Mountain Herd the day after you received your power. He said he couldn't trust a betrayer."

Morningleaf snorted. "I'll agree with that."

Brackentail continued. "His captain, Frostfire, escorted me to the Vein, and . . ." He paused, then exhaled long and slow. "He kicked me, broke my wing, and left me to die."

Morningleaf stamped her hoof. "You don't expect us to feel bad about that, do you?"

"Morningleaf!" Star glanced at her, surprised to see her amber eyes crackling with anger.

"No," Brackentail answered her. "I deserved it for what I did." He raised his head, and the slits of his eyes glistened with tears. "But Rockwing lied. I didn't help him win the war. I . . . I wouldn't do that, Morningleaf." He looked directly at the filly, his eyes pleading. "I knew

Silverlake was holding meetings at the waterfall. I knew she was going to try to save the black foal." Brackentail nodded toward Star. "I believed he was dangerous. I was trying to save Sun Herd, and all the pegasi of Anok, from him."

Morningleaf whinnied sharply, her feathers vibrating. "That's no excuse! You should have spoken to my sire, not to Rockwing." Morningleaf charged forward, eye to eye with the brown colt. "Do you know how many Sun Herd pegasi died in the battle?"

Brackentail shrank away from her.

"Their blood is on your wings *forever*!" Morningleaf stamped away from him, breathing fast and hard.

"It wasn't planned," whinnied Brackentail. "I was captured."

Morningleaf whirled on him, teeth bared. "So you betrayed your herd to save yourself?"

Brackentail's thin-slit eyes widened slightly.

"Brackentail," Star interrupted. "You're making things worse. Just tell us why you're here. What do you want?"

Brackentail stared up at the clouds drifting overhead. "I have nowhere else to go."

"So you want to join River Herd?"

The colt nodded.

"No," whinnied Morningleaf. "Absolutely not."

Star touched her back with his wing. Her entire body was trembling. "We'll bring it to the council and let them decide."

She faced him. "You can't be serious."

"If we leave him here, he'll die."

Morningleaf pinned her ears. "That's not our problem."

"He's asking for our protection. And look at him; he's harmless."

"He's harmless *now*, but he helped Rockwing destroy us, and he didn't do anything to protect Echofrost." Star knew that. Echofrost was Morningleaf's friend, and when Brackentail tried to kill Star in a canyon run moons ago, Mountain Herd steeds had captured her and Brackentail. The brown colt worked with his captors, giving them information about Sun Herd, while poor Echofrost had been tortured and then released.

Morningleaf reared, charging Brackentail again, halting just short of ramming him. "Everything you feared Star would do to Sun Herd—*you* did!"

Brackentail collapsed under her accusations.

13